The kiss started deep, shattering her self-control...

Samantha knew then that she wanted to make love to this man, fast and furious, slow and sensual, both ways, all ways....

Luc made a sound low in his throat. The rumbling growl didn't sound completely human.

She opened her eyes and blinked. Thousands of glittering fireflies suddenly swirled in a frenetic dance before her face. *No. Not possible.* She backed away.

Surrounded by flickering light, Luc made another sound, an animal cry, and tore away into the woods.

Despite her fear, Sam followed. The snow was deep enough that she could step into his tracks. Turning a slow circle, she realized the footprints stopped...and animal tracks appeared. *Wolf prints.*

A snuffling noise made her turn. A majestic, pewter-colored wolf waited.

KAREN WHIDDON

Though she doesn't howl at the moon, Karen Whiddon swears she can sometimes communicate with wolves' close relatives—dogs. Her two fur-faced children are her closest friends. Having grown up in the Catskills and the Rockies, she enjoys shadowy forests and snow-capped mountains. Her hobbies include camping and fishing. In addition to writing, she works full-time as vice president of a commercial insurance agency and makes her home with her wonderful husband and two canine companions.

You can contact Karen by e-mail via her Web site, KarenWhiddon.com, or by snail mail at P.O. Box 820807, Fort Worth, TX 76172.

TOUCH OF THE WOLF

KAREN WHIDDON

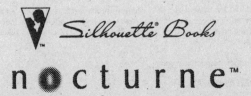

Silhouette Books

nocturne™

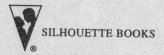

SILHOUETTE BOOKS

ISBN-13: 978-0-373-61759-3
ISBN-10:   0-373-61759-3

TOUCH OF THE WOLF

www.silhouettenocturne.com

Printed in U.S.A.

Dear Reader,

Healing seems to be a reoccurring theme throughout my stories. We all have hidden chasms inside of us, emotional scars from which we never quite recover. I firmly believe love can heal most of those chasms, and I enjoy writing about such a healing power. In *Touch of the Wolf* you'll meet Samantha Warren, who has the miraculous gift of healing animals with a touch, and Luc Herrick, a man who no longer believes in miracles.

Travel with me back to Anniversary, Texas, and Leaning Tree, New York, magical places where anything can happen. The people in my fictional towns are very dear to me. Getting to visit both places in one story was really exciting, especially when reconnecting with characters like Carson and Brenna Turner from *One Eye Open,* and Alex and Lyssa Lupe from *One Eye Closed.* Jewel and Colton Reynolds from *Cry of the Wolf* make an appearance, as well.

I hope you enjoy reading about Sam and Luc's journey, both toward love and toward healing, and come away with a better sense that life may not always be as it appears.

Sincerely,

Karen Whiddon

This book is dedicated to all the wonderful editors
at Harlequin/Silhouette who've believed in me and
helped make my stories better—Leslie Wainger,
Tara Gavin, Patience Smith, Jessica Alvarez
and most of all, my wonderful editor extraordinaire
Natashya Wilson. Tashya, you have a keen eye
and a kind heart. Working with you is like
a dream come true. Thank you.

Chapter 1

He'd come to Texas to find a healer, not a mate.

Appalled and shocked, Lucaine Herrick stared at the beautiful woman who might or might not be able to save his best friend's dying little girl.

Samantha Warren. Potential healer.

He wanted to howl. To change, right then and there. To shed his human skin and feel the damp earth beneath his paws, the coiled power in his limbs; to give himself over to nothing but muscle and sinew. To run, his strength pushing him faster, harder.

Instead, he met her gaze and smiled. Smiled as

though his heart wasn't pounding. As though he didn't recognize her.

If she was what his Pack suggested, a healer, then she was rarest of rare, the stuff of legends. A human woman, half shifter; a Halfling who couldn't change, who was unable to become wolf. One look at her told him she had no idea of that. She didn't know the power she had, the potential for great good residing within her.

He did.

Worse, in that first second when their gazes met, he'd known what else she was.

She was his mate.

No. Yet how could even a man who'd sworn never to marry deny the one woman created only for him?

Easily, he told himself. He had to be mistaken. Kyle's death and the subsequent illness of three-year-old Lucy had combined to rob him of reason and common sense. After all, his doctorate in psychology had taught him there were deep-seated reasons for most delusions. True love ranked up there with the worst of them as far as he was concerned.

Thus armed, he moved closer to the unsuspecting woman. Even here, in this crowded café, the lure of her pulled at him. How could this be? She was a redhead, while he preferred brunettes. Tall and slender and willowy, while he favored petite and curvy. The exotic tilt of her caramel-colored eyes might be lovely, though in the past he'd always liked blue eyes.

Samantha Warren was the antithesis of everything he found desirable in a woman, yet he could not deny her beauty. He took a deep breath, striving for steadiness, for calm. Her beauty was normal. After all, most Halflings were blessed with extraordinary good looks.

Yet never had a Halfling appealed to him as much as this one did. Hell, no *woman* had ever made him shake with the need to touch her. All because she was his mate, destined to be with him always.

Superstitious nonsense. Giving himself a stern talking-to, he took the stool next to her at the crowded café counter. He inhaled again and managed to give her a nonchalant nod before pretending to turn his attention to the breakfast menu. This close, he could taste her scent, sweet like honey, exotically tinged with citrus. Sexy. Again he battled the desire to touch her, to learn if her creamy skin felt as soft as it looked.

Hell hounds. He'd come to this small Texas town on a mission. He couldn't afford to let a pretty face distract him.

Scowling, he forced himself to remember the grief-stricken expression his best friend, Carson, had worn when he'd given Luc the news about Lucy, Luc's godchild and the daughter Carson had named after him.

Painful.

"Hey, surely the menu isn't that bad, is it?"

Even her voice affected him, sending chills down the length of his spine. Looking up, he met her gaze, bracing himself against the onslaught of sensation, the fierce rush of need and want and longing.

"Pardon me?"

She smiled, the effect of which had him clenching his fists to keep from reaching for her. "You were giving the menu such a black look, I thought I'd offer you my breakfast recommendation. I eat here all the time, so I promise I'm well qualified to suggest something good."

Struck dumb for the first time in his life, Luc swallowed, trying to gather his thoughts. "What do you recommend?" he asked, his voice sounded more like a growl than he'd intended.

Her lovely eyes widened, but she bravely leaned close, pointing to an item on the menu labeled "King's Breakfast." Luc barely suppressed a shudder when her long hair brushed over his arm.

Soft. So soft.

"This one is excellent. Lots of meat—protein. Of course, if you're not a meat eater—"

"I am." Was it his imagination, or had her voice softened, becoming breathless? Again, sharp desire stabbed him, waking his wolf.

Not good. Not good at all.

Ruthlessly, he forced away his need. He had a short time frame to learn the truth about this woman, or Lucy would die. He couldn't allow lust to come between him and his quest. And lust had to be all this was. Finding his mate had no place in the scheme of things. Finding a healer did.

When the waitress came, he placed an order for the King's Breakfast. Samantha did the same, chatting easily with the stocky woman in the pink, polyester uniform. When the woman moved off, Samantha turned her attention back to Luc. He felt the full force of her amber gaze like a punch to the gut.

"What brings you to Anniversary?" Smiling pleasantly, she seemed completely unaware of her effect on him. "Are you just passing through, or…?"

Now came the part he'd been dreading—his cover story. Luc hated lies, hated liars even worse. If he'd been allowed to choose, he would have barged in, confronted Samantha and hauled her back to Leaning Tree, New York, on the first available flight. Even if the rumors proved false, if there was the remotest chance she could help Lucy, he'd take it.

His plan had been voted down. Though the Pack council felt otherwise, it wasn't until they'd pointed out that healers couldn't ever be forced to heal that Luc had reluctantly acceded to their wishes.

"I'm here to investigate the werewolf sightings," he said, watching her eyes widen. "I've a meeting with a Samantha Warren at the library in—" he made a show of consulting his watch "—one hour."

"You're Dr. Herrick?"

At his nod, she held out her hand, laughing slightly, inviting him to share in the joke. "What an odd coincidence, running into you here. I'm Samantha Warren. Looks like our meeting just got moved up."

Unable to tear his gaze away from her face, he slid his fingers around hers. Her skin was as smooth as he'd imagined, and he tightened his grip. With a puzzled tilt of her head, she stiffened, as if his touch had shocked her.

Despite that, he kept her hand securely in his.

Color bloomed in her face, her pale skin suffusing with rose. The urge to kiss her seized him—

he actually tugged on her hand to pull her to him before realizing he was about to make a serious mistake, a fatal error.

Instead, he released her, forcing what he hoped was a pleasant smile on his face. "Wonderful. I'm so glad to meet you. I can't tell you how grateful I am for your kind offer of help."

She regarded him gravely, an unsettled expression flitting across her beautiful face. "No thanks are necessary—that's what I do. Librarians and authors are always a good fit."

Fascinated, he watched her blush deepen, as she realized the possible meaning of her words. They *would* be a good fit, if they were true mates, he thought. She'd sheath him as tightly as a glove, while he'd fill her with— His body instantly hardened.

Damn.

"More coffee?" The waitress returned, refilling their cups without waiting for an answer. "Your breakfasts should be out shortly."

Unable to tear his gaze from Samantha, he nodded, and the woman moved away.

Blinking, Samantha shook her head as if awakening from a dream. "What were we talking about?"

"Your help with my research for this book."

"Oh, yes. You'll be glad to know I carry all of your books in our library here. The one on the Loch Ness Monster is a particular favorite with middle-schoolers."

He barely registered her words. The only thought that consumed him was the need to cover her mouth with his and taste her lips. And more.

Breathing raggedly, he felt absurdly grateful when the waitress slid their breakfast platters in front of them with much clinking of silverware and china.

Samantha, too, appeared relieved, focusing on the meal in front of her.

For the next several minutes, Luc concentrated on his food, praying his body would settle down. The intensity of his reaction to her was far outside the realm of his experience.

The only family member who'd already found his mate was— Savagely, he bit off the thought. He missed Kyle. His younger half brother had married young, announcing to the entire Pack that Shannon was his mate. The two had been one of the happiest couples Luc had ever seen, until the illness claimed Kyle's life. Now Shannon barely existed, a shadow of her formerly vibrant self.

Luc could identify. His biggest regret was his

inability to help his beloved brother, despite his doctoral degree. Instead, he'd been forced to slowly watch him die.

If Samantha Warren was truly a healer, discovery of her abilities had come too late to help Kyle.

A healer. When his doorbell had rung at eleven forty-five one night a week ago, he'd been surprised to find a member of the Leaning Tree Pack Council on his doorstep.

"We're calling an immediate council meeting," Joe O'Toole had said. "Meet us down at city hall in half an hour."

"It's nearly midnight. What's the emergency?"

But the man had already moved off and didn't answer.

At city hall, Luc had been shocked to find half the town in attendance. Council meetings were always open forums, but with the timing and rush-rush nature of this one, he would have thought most people would have waited to read about it the next day in the paper.

Frank Mahoney, who as mayor also served as head of the council, opened the meeting. "We've received some wonderful and disturbing news. We may have found a healer."

The gathering erupted in noise. Such a thing

would be almost a miracle; no healers had existed in this generation, nor the two before.

When the racket died down, Frank had continued. "As many of you know, the Barerras just returned from visiting relatives in Texas. Tomas Barerra changed and got caught in some kind of trap. Then, when he was fighting to get free, another wolf attacked him. Tomas thinks it was another shifter, but he couldn't be sure. He was already wounded and completely unprepared. The wolf ripped him to pieces and left him to die."

Luc had stood. "Tomas is only a kid. Where were his parents?"

"He's nine, Luc. He sneaked off to have a change and romp through the woods. He had no idea there was any danger. Neither did they. Even when they realized he was missing, they weren't too worried."

"As you are aware, if he'd been full-blooded, he would have healed." Samuel Moss, another council member, had picked up the story. "But since he's a Halfling, he couldn't heal himself. Tomas says a human male found him, still in his wolf form, and took him to an animal doctor. She called in another woman, one who touched him.

"He said he felt heat, a warmth spreading

through him. A moment later, his wounds were gone, as was his pain. He was healed, just like in the texts of old. His parents saw the blood, the scars. This woman in Texas must be a healer. What else can it be?"

Again shouts of jubilation mingled with chatter. Frank gave the crowd a pleased smile. "We've unanimously decided Luc Herrick, as town psychologist, must go to Texas and investigate."

Of course. Though still hurting over his brother's untimely death, he'd been given the task of finding someone and something he didn't even believe could be real. To him, a healer was merely an abstract concept, not a possible reality. At best, a myth. After all, if healers *were* real, why hadn't God sent Samantha Warren in time to help Kyle?

He knew why they'd asked him. He had no family here, not anymore. In their own way they thought this trip might help him heal—as a practicing psychologist, objectively he knew they were right.

In the end he agreed to go because he needed something to do. Something to distract him. Maybe this had shown, too—the restless anger, the crippling feelings of inadequacy—all of this might be helped with a trip out of town. A quest.

Though privately, Luc believed they were wasting their time.

When the meeting finally ended a half hour later, he'd gone home and packed. The plane ticket Frank had pressed into his hand showed he was flying out in the morning.

On the long flight heading southwest, Luc had read the dry and dusty books he'd packed in his carry-on. His seating companion, a teenage girl who'd eyed the scholarly tomes with disinterest before opening her fashion magazine, completely ignored him. This made researching an easier task.

Nearly every text had something definitive to say on healers, but the material disturbed him. Instead of treating healers with healthy skepticism, the books discussed them as if they were not only an actuality, but constantly born into existence, if one searched diligently enough.

Worse, each book agreed on the details of the delusion. Healers were always born Halflings, and most of them questioned why they couldn't change. They all performed healings first on small animals, both wild and domestic, before moving up to Halflings. Training honed their skills, but no one, from Pack scientists to Pack doctors, had been able to learn how their healing ability worked. Thus, they were considered blessed.

Luc had closed the last volume with a wry smile. Maybe the next book he wrote would debunk this particular myth. Though it could be published only within the Pack, he'd consider it a community service.

Belatedly, he realized Samantha Warren had pushed away her plate, while he'd barely touched his breakfast. Suddenly ravenous, he devoured his eggs, bacon, sausage and ham, leaving the pancakes and toast uneaten.

She watched him with apparent fascination.

"Very nice," he told her when he'd finished. "Thank you for the suggestion." Then, waving away her protests, he proceeded to pay for both their meals.

She was his, after all.

Angered at the unwanted thought, Luc pocketed the check and steeled himself to look at her. He could only hope he was successful at hiding the fierce desire she made him feel.

"Would you like to follow me to the library?" Her troubled expression told him she didn't relish the idea of further contact with him. "We open in twenty minutes."

He nodded, holding the door for her. She took great care not to brush against him when she walked past, a move he noted and both regretted and relished, because he now knew she felt the connection as well.

Walking to her car with the tall, dark stranger behind her, Sam felt as though she was being stalked. Hunted, like prey. Dismissing her fears as irrational—after all, Dr. Lucaine Herrick enjoyed a stellar reputation as an author and a clinical psychologist—she kept her head high and her steps brisk. She didn't like that she had to force herself not to look over her shoulder at him. And she sure as heck didn't like her body's unwanted response to his slightest touch.

Aroused, wanton, out of control.

Around him, she felt like a bitch in heat.

Feeling her face heat even at the thought, she started her car and pulled onto the street. A dark blue sedan fell in behind her.

The ten-block trip took longer than usual as she drove exactly the speed limit, hoping the delay would give her time to get herself together.

Her reaction to this man defied comprehension. True, Luc Herrick was handsome, in a dark, mysterious way, but ever since the plane crash and Eric's departure from their marriage and her life, she hadn't been looking. Not even for a one-night stand. Sex and she had parted on unfriendly terms, especially with her ex's hateful assessment of her as a dried up, barren nonwoman.

The death of her mother from the crash and her own injuries—both emotional and physical—had ensured she'd never be fit to be any man's woman or wife. Eric had made that perfectly clear. What kind of man would tie himself to a woman who couldn't have children?

Parking in the spot reserved for her, Sam took a deep breath and climbed out of her Volkswagen. In the sky high above, a jet flew past, making her shudder in remembrance. Grabbing the car door, she concentrated on breathing, slow and steady, as she'd been taught. Yet again, though eighteen months had passed since the plane crash, she felt herself plummeting to the ground, heard the awful screams of terror, felt the bone-jarring jolt right before impact.

Beyond that, she remembered little. They'd told her she'd crawled from the burning wreckage, with two broken ribs and cuts and scrapes. Most of her fellow passengers had not survived, including the only family she had, her beloved mother.

Samantha herself should be dead. This thought came again for the hundredth time. Survivor's guilt. Their seats had been side by side. She didn't understand why she'd survived, while her mother had perished. And the penalty she'd paid, the loss of her marriage, the knowledge she'd never bear a child, often seemed too much to bear.

Wincing, she straightened and swung her door closed, pressing her remote once to lock it.

"Are you all right?"

His deep voice made her jump. Pressing a hand to her throat, she nodded, carefully avoiding looking at him. "Of course."

She kept her tone professional, businesslike, even though her heart raced. "Please, follow me inside and I'll see you have access to any materials you need."

As they walked toward the main entrance, he took her arm. "Wait."

Again, the sensations. She wanted to lean into his embrace and rub against him like a stray kitten hungry for his caresses. Horrified, she jerked away, breathing fast. Her physical reaction was bad enough, but for a second, she'd even seen the wolves she used to dream about. Unable to keep her stark emotions from showing in her eyes, she glanced quickly at him, then away. "What?"

"Tell me about your werewolf."

"Not *my* werewolf. I've never seen it." Jiggling her keys in her hand, she asked a question of her own. "How did you learn about it, way up north?"

"Your paper ran a story and the affiliates picked it up. I read the story in the *Times* and immediately knew I had to come and see for myself. All those missing pets combined with werewolf sightings make good fodder for one of my books, especially since I write about supernatural phenomena."

"I know." She resisted the urge to tap her foot in impatience. The library opened in four minutes and she needed to be inside or she'd ruin her ten-year record of never being late. "I've read them."

When he didn't respond, she again chanced a sideways glance at him. He watched her with an intensity that felt as darkly disturbing as it was thrilling.

"I've made a career of investigating myths. Thus far, each and every one of them has turned out to be false."

"This one definitely is." Nerves still on edge, she gave him a tight smile. "There are no such things as werewolves."

"So you don't believe in it?"

"The supposed werewolf? No." She unlocked the door, yanking it open and stepping inside. Motioning Luc to follow, she headed down the carpeted hallway to her office. Even here, in the back hallways off-limits to the public, the hushed quality she'd always loved reigned supreme.

She lowered her voice. "Though quite a few people claim to have seen it, I think it's probably just some high school kids playing a prank."

"Could be." Keeping pace with her, he didn't sound concerned. "But then what about the missing pets?"

"Now that I can't explain."

"Yet you still think this werewolf is a prank?"

Hesitantly, she nodded.

"Well, I guess I won't really know until I check it out fully."

"You plan to prove this werewolf is false?"

"Yes." He smiled, again delivering that flash of heat. "Of course. Everyone knows there are no such things, right?"

The way he watched her told her that for some reason, her answer was important to him. She shook her head. "There is no werewolf here. If you're hoping to find one, you're wasting your time."

"Maybe. Either way, I'll get another book out

of this. This one will be the third in my series on paranormal frauds."

"How long are you planning to stay in Anniversary?"

He shrugged. "As long as it takes."

Something about his answer sent a shiver down her spine.

Checking her watch, she realized if she didn't hurry and get to her office, she'd consider herself late. Increasing her pace, she made a right turn, then a left, before depositing her purse on her desk.

Nine o'clock. Whew.

Behind her, Luc cleared his throat.

"Have a seat." Waving him to a chair, she sat at her desk and then logged on to her computer. "What were we talking about again?" She knew it hadn't been how badly she wanted to jump his bones.

"The werewolf."

Ah. "So you're hoping the story is false, right?" She couldn't help but admire him as he folded his tall body into one of her chairs.

"No, this time, I'm actually hoping it's real. I'd love to discover a paranormal anomaly." His wry smile made her wonder about his private joke, though she didn't know him well enough to ask.

Dropping her purse into her desk drawer, she

nodded. "I don't think you need to worry about that possibility."

"You definitely don't believe in shape-shifters?" Again the intense look.

"No."

"Interesting, with your special abilities and all."

Sam froze. "What?"

He leaned forward, pinning her with his dark gaze. "I was told you helped heal a dying wolf pup that had been mauled by the werewolf about a week ago."

Chapter 2

*T*old? She could only hope her voice sounded steady. "I have no idea what you're talking about."

His unwavering gaze seemed to mark her a liar. "About two weeks ago, you healed a dying wolf pup that was injured in a rusty old trap, or so I've heard."

Deep breath. Forcing herself to smile normally, she shook her head. "Nope, not me. I'd say someone's been gossiping, just like they do about that werewolf."

"Is the gossip true?"

Crap. Surely he could see her pulse pounding

in the hollow of her throat. Still, no way was she admitting anything to this handsome stranger. "True? How could it be?" She forced a laugh. "As usual with gossip, the story's complete nonsense."

"No wolf pup?" Was that disappointment in his face?

"Yes, there was a hurt wolf pup. He was brought in to the veterinary clinic. My best friend, Patricia Lelane, is the town vet. *She* saved the animal, not me. I was there, so I helped. You might want to talk to her. She'll confirm that for you."

"Thanks, I will."

"Where did you hear this nonsense?" Only Patricia knew the truth. And Patricia would never tell.

"When I called the police department I had a long conversation with the dispatcher."

Hilda Ramos. Another one who'd claimed to have glimpsed the werewolf. "I see."

"She said Charles Pentworth told her he found a dying wolf pup and took it to the vet's to be euthanized."

"Charles?" She dismissed him with a gesture, relief enabling her to catch her breath. "He also claims he's seen this werewolf several times. Don't put any credence in what he says."

"He runs the bank. From what I can tell, he's a respectable, responsible citizen."

"He is, but—"

"Charles also told me," Luc interrupted, "that the next thing he knew, Patricia claimed the mortally wounded wolf pup had healed—and escaped."

Maybe Sam could distract him and gain an answer to the question that had plagued her for so long. "Was that wolf pup your pet? Are you the one who broke into the clinic and stole him?"

One corner of his mouth lifted. "No. I'm sure he let himself out."

Was this man kidding? "Let himself out? Please."

"You said you'd help me. I need you to tell me how you healed him. What did you do? Did you touch him?" Herrick's intent stare made her feel as if he really did know her secret. But he didn't. He couldn't.

For the first time since meeting him, she felt an icy slice of fear. Not *of* him, but of what he might inadvertently learn. "People can't heal just by touch."

He shook his shaggy head, an odd expression on his craggy face. "If you only understood how important this is. I need to find a healer."

The statement floored her. All she could do, all she could think, was *run*. Immediately.

Of course she wouldn't.

"A healer." She felt as though she were choking. The word felt foreign on her tongue. Strange, but oddly right, too.

"Yes. Are you?" His intent gaze seemed to plead with her to tell him the truth.

As if. "I'm not a miracle worker," she told him quietly. "I'm just a small-town girl who works as a librarian. Look, I don't mind helping you research this supposed werewolf, but you need to promise to leave me alone."

"Leave you alone? In what way?"

"Bugging me about this healing stuff. Thinking I can bring animals back from the dead."

"I never said that." One corner of his mouth lifted in a smile. "But I'll tell you what, Samantha Warren. If that's what you want, I promise I won't ask you again without justification. Agreed?"

"Yes." She felt quite certain she wouldn't be giving him any reasons. "And you can call me Sam. Everyone does."

"Sam then. I'm Luc."

The abbreviation sounded much more sensual than his full name. She didn't even want to say it out loud, not with her emotions running so close to out of control.

Unable to look away, even though she felt desire coiling low in her belly, she asked a question she'd sworn she wouldn't ask. "Then what? If and when you find this werewolf, what happens after?"

"I write my book."

"And?"

"I leave town." One dark brow rose. "Of course."

Of course.

Pushing himself out of the chair, he prowled her small office, as if lost in thought. She watched him, admiring his lithe grace and long-legged stride.

"Tell me about what you do," she asked.

"Do?" He glanced at her over his shoulder, making her realize again just how striking and sensual his unusual looks were. With his long dark hair and strong features, his masculine beauty tugged at her at a level far deeper than mere sexual attraction.

Want. Need. Desire. A sense of belonging.

All things she craved.

Not good.

Belatedly, she realized he waited for her to answer. "Yes, do. As in the books you write. What made you choose such an...odd profession?"

"You find writers odd?"

"Not that. What you choose to write about.

How did you get into writing about such fantastical things?"

He shrugged. "The world is much more full and varied than you humans realize."

You humans? A shiver ran down her spine and she wondered whether to let that one go, or ask.

When he saw her hesitation, one corner of his mouth quirked in a smile. "There are many species of sentient beings, more than you realize."

Her laugh sounded uneasy, even to her own ears. "First you try to get me to believe in werewolves, and now you're telling me there are others?"

"Of course."

Despite the fact that they were playing—she thought—she couldn't contain her curiosity. "Vampires? Ghosts?"

"Yes. And faeries, elves and dwarfs. In addition to what you call werewolves, there are shifters for most large animal breeds. Birds, too. And dolphins."

Though he sounded serious, she knew there was no way he could be. Not and write nonfiction books debunking the very things they discussed.

"What about mermaids?" She'd always loved the idea of being able to breathe under the sea.

"And mermen. They call themselves mer-people."

She waited for him to laugh, or say something to

indicate he was joking. When he didn't, she shook her head. "I don't believe in any of that supernatural nonsense. I mean, shape-shifters and vampires defy logic. Any reasonable person would know—"

"That things exist that cannot be explained."

She stared. "You sound as though you believe."

"I do."

"But you write books discrediting them."

"There are some things I haven't been able to disprove."

Again, she decided it was safer to let his statement go. "Just don't try to convince me or make me believe in your reality, okay? I'm perfectly happy in my own normal little world."

"Are you?" The heat in his gaze seared her, making her mouth go dry. Again she could feel her heart rate increase; again she fought the baffling urge to touch him.

No way was she going down that road.

"Yes," she said firmly. "I am."

"I see." He studied her, making her feel as though he could see into her soul. "I think I'd better go."

"What about the reference books?"

"I'll take a rain check." With another of those fast, amazing smiles, he turned and left.

Expelling breath she hadn't even realized she was holding, Sam leaned on her desk, shaken. She felt wrung out like a wet dishrag, as if Lucaine Herrick had zapped her energy like some sort of vampire.

Great. Now even she was doing it. First a werewolf running around town and now this. Vampire? What would be next? Zombies and ghouls?

Shaking her head, she gave herself a mental slap. Whatever feelings Luc Herrick aroused in her were unwanted and unnecessary. She refused to even think about them. Not today, not ever. She'd had enough of that kind of thing to last a lifetime.

Taking a deep breath, she called Patricia and filled her in. "He asked me about healing the wolf pup."

Patricia's sharp intake of breath reassured her. "How did he…"

"Charles Pentworth," they both said at once.

"It could be worse." Patricia kept her normally brisk voice soothing. "Unless they're squarely in the I-believe-in-werewolves camp, no one pays attention to Charles."

"Luc Herrick did."

"He didn't know any better. Don't worry about him."

"Patricia, he's an author. He's here to research the town werewolf."

"Ever since we made the newspaper…"

"I know."

"Did he seem…I don't know, like some sort of weirdo?"

"No," Sam admitted. "He seemed respectable. He's a psychologist." And attractive as hell, in a darkly sensual, mysterious way, though Sam didn't tell Patricia that. "He writes nonfiction books debunking myths like this. But I was shocked when he asked me about healing the wolf pup."

"I don't think he can do any damage."

"Good, because people are already panicking about this supposed werewolf. I don't want to freak them out any more."

"Just keep steering him toward the werewolf believers. There are enough of them to keep him busy and out of your hair."

"Good idea." Sam sighed, thinking. "Werewolves. Who would believe such a thing? I don't know what they saw or why, but some locals honestly believe there's a genuine werewolf running around in the woods. As long as they continue to insist some man changed into a wolf, they'll have plenty to talk about."

"Especially Charles Pentworth."

"And Hilda Ramos. Shawn Ferguson. Oh, and let's not forget the Ater sisters."

"Mass hysteria." Patricia sighed. "Though I have to say, Charles is one of the most levelheaded people I know. If he says he saw it, I'm almost inclined to believe he did."

Sam rubbed her eyes. "Don't tell me you think—?"

"Of course not. There's got to be some trick to this. Illusion or special effects. But why? Too much doesn't add up. First various townspeople claim to have seen a werewolf. Next, a young wolf is hurt here, in Anniversary. We never get wolves out here. Coyotes, maybe. The occasional bobcat. But no wolves."

She paused for breath. "Now, people's pets are disappearing and turning up dead. Eaten. And the very wolf cub that was so out of place appeared to have been attacked by a larger, more powerful wolf. To top all this strange stuff off, the recuperating wolf pup escaped a closed cage and a locked building and left, closing the door after himself. There's simply no explanation. Except…"

"Not realistic." Stomach hurting, Sam crossed her arms.

"You know and I know," Patricia sighed. "There are no such things as werewolves. A man becoming a wolf is not medically possible. The anatomies are too dissimilar."

"Then how did this wolf escape?"

"Most likely the same people who, for whatever reason, are going around trying to make everyone believe they're werewolves, are involved."

"That's the most likely scenario."

"Who knows?" Patricia sounded frustrated. "Whatever happened, I don't like it. I still want to know how that wolf pup escaped, and where he is now."

Still clutching the phone, Sam snagged a mug and poured herself a cup of coffee. The library was open, though her first meeting wasn't for another half hour and she needed to get her caffeine fix before then. "If Luc Herrick comes around asking questions, don't tell him anything."

"Of course I won't. Look, I've got to let you go. My staff's here, along with the first patient of the day."

After clicking off the phone, Sam sipped her coffee and tried to think.

Werewolves. While she knew they didn't exist, when talk had started around town, she'd gotten chills. Mostly because she'd dreamed of wolves ever since she was a small child. She even used to pretend she could magically become a wolf. Like a werewolf.

When a group of hysterical teenagers had claimed to see a man changing into a wolf in one of the untamed, wooded areas near the lake, most people had dismissed their claims, figuring they'd been smoking weed or drinking. They'd pooh-poohed the story.

Until Charles Pentworth stepped forward and backed them up. He'd seen the werewolf, too, on numerous occasions, he claimed. He hadn't said anything until now because he feared people would consider him crazy.

At that, the gossip had escalated. The town had divided into two camps. Some said Charles *was* crazy, and wanted to know what he was doing lurking in the woods. Stress must have gotten to him, causing him to see things that weren't there.

Others, knowing Charles to be the most analytical mind in seven counties, seemed inclined to believe him. After all, he ran the First Savings and Loan Bank and sat on the city council. People believed his words lent credence to the kids' claim.

Sam tried to stay out of the fray. So did Patricia.

Privately, they'd both wondered about motive. Why would someone try to convince an entire town he was a werewolf? What were his plans?

Then Hilda Ramos had a sighting. She'd been the police dispatcher for years and was well-liked and well-respected.

The town had been divided squarely ever since. Debates ran hot and heavy between those who believed in the werewolf and those who didn't, proving once again that the age-old complaint of teenagers was accurate: there really wasn't enough to do in a small town like Anniversary.

Keeping to the shadows of the forest that ringed the lake, he wavered between human and wolf. Most humans thought him a myth. The Pack wanted to keep things that way and would be furious once they learned he'd allowed human strangers to see him change.

Michael didn't care. He wasn't Pack, he was Outside. Sickness ravaged his body and the disease affected his mind. He knew he was dying. When he'd heard a rumor of a Halfling with power, a Halfling like himself, he'd come to this small community southeast of Dallas on the slim chance the rumors were true.

A dying man grasped at any straw.

Thus far, though he watched the woman night and day, he'd seen nothing to lend the stories credence. Yet he wouldn't give up, couldn't give up. If the slightest chance existed that her touch could make him well, he'd claim her healing power for his own. The one who controlled a true healer could rule not only the Pack, but the world.

When his cell phone rang as he climbed into his rental car, Luc knew who was calling without looking at the caller ID. Sometimes his days were like that.

"Checking up on me?"

The mayor of Leaning Tree chuckled. "Maybe. The entire town's excited. You know how it is. Everyone's talking, and they want me to keep them apprised of your progress."

"I've only been here two days."

"Time enough to learn the truth. So tell me, is she a healer?"

"I don't know."

Frank let his exasperation sound in his voice, which was unlike him. A true politician, he rarely showed any emotion besides enthusiasm. "Can't you simply ask her?"

"I did. She said no. Even worse, if this woman is a healer, she has no idea about her heritage. She knows nothing about shifters or the Pack."

Frank's shocked silence said what the normally garrulous man thought of *that*.

"I'm afraid this is going to take longer than we thought," Luc warned, running his free hand through his hair. "I can't just bulldoze in and expect her to believe me."

The sharp hiss of breath on the other end of the line was answer enough. "Lucy doesn't have that much time."

"Believe me, I know that."

"Are you *sure* she doesn't know?"

"Absolutely. If she can do what Tomas Barerra says she can, she must think she has some sort of gift. That is, if she really can heal." He let his dubious tone speak for itself. "I've seen no proof, so far. I'm not sure I've actually found a healer here." His chest ached at the thought. If Sam wasn't one, Lucy would die.

Frank sighed. "Ask her about Tomas."

"I did. She's admitted nothing. All everyone is talking about around here is the werewolf who's been lurking in the woods."

"You mentioned that. What is he? A rogue shifter?"

"Maybe. I'm looking into it. One thing for sure, he gave me a perfect reason to be in town. You know everyone's been wanting me to write a book debunking werewolves."

"True, true." The other man chuckled. "More protection for us. Every time some book or movie proves we're not real, we benefit. Imagine how old Bessie up in Loch Ness feels."

Luc grinned. His book on the so-called Loch Ness Monster had been a rousing success. "Still," he said, sobering, "I don't understand why this shifter is skulking around town. He's frightening them."

"It's been a while since I've heard about a rogue anywhere, except for that serial killer a few years back."

They both fell silent, remembering. One of Luc's friends, Alex Lupe, had nearly lost his wife Lyssa to that killer.

Clearing his throat, Frank continued. "These days, everyone has some Pack affiliation. Have you talked to the Texas Pack? They're the ones who helped compile the information on Sam Warren."

"Yes. They know nothing about who he is or why he's revealing himself to humans. They've asked me to check into it also. If this is a true rogue, he's in their jurisdiction. They'll have to handle him."

"We don't need complications." Frank sounded weary. "All I want is for you to bring home this healer. Brenna and Carson—heck, our entire town—need some fresh hope."

Hope had come too late for Luc's brother. Closing his eyes against the familiar, piercing pain, he didn't tell the mayor that he still had times where he picked up the phone to call and started dialing the number, before realizing Kyle was gone. Though Kyle'd been his half brother and a Halfling to boot, they'd grown up together and been best friends. Luc missed him more than words could say.

"I don't know about her, Frank. I've met her, spent time with her. She admits nothing."

"You asked her, straight-out?" The mayor sounded incredulous. Probably because he knew Luc better that that.

"Yes." Dragging his hand through his hair, Luc tried to explain his feelings. "She's…different."

"Of course she's different!" The normally placid man exploded. "She's a healer. They're rare. I don't understand the problem."

"We don't know she's a healer." Though he

realized he sounded cynical, Luc hated how everyone in Leaning Tree had taken a nine-year-old boy's word and instantly believed in miracles. Luc knew better. He'd like to have a chat with the lad's parents. Nothing like getting an entire town's hopes up and then leaving him to quash them.

And then Carson and Brenna and Lucy. Thinking about the hope they insisted on clinging to made him want to weep.

Sometimes Luc hated his job. Especially lately.

He tried again. "You don't understand—you haven't met her. There's something about her...." He swallowed, knowing he couldn't tell the other man about the persistent feeling that she was his mate.

"Go on."

Luc took a deep breath. He had to try. "She's...disturbing." To say the least.

"So she could be a healer then?"

At the bald excitement in Frank's voice, Luc winced. "I don't know. Not necessarily. I can find no signs that she even knows she's a Halfling."

"So you've said. But what about the desire to change? If she is a Halfling, unless someone is suppressing it, she has to know. Unless..."

Unless she *was* truly a healer. Legend said

healers were never able to change. They channeled that energy into healing instead.

And Sam claimed not to believe in shape-shifters.

Frank concluded the call by asking if Luc needed anything, as though he planned to send a care package full of charitable goods. While Luc appreciated him asking, he told the other man he was fine.

Taking a deep breath, he collected his thoughts. Now to find Sam without appearing to stalk her, even though he was. The irony of it all made him grimace. Within the Pack, Luc held the honor of top hunter. He found his prey more quickly, made the cleanest kills, and his skill was legendary. Yet he questioned his ability to do this. Hunting a human woman felt far different than hunting a deer or rabbit as a wolf. Especially when he had to fight the sensation that she was his mate.

Chapter 3

"I called the adoption agency again." Sam stirred her drink, touching her tongue to the salty rim before taking a sip. Los Hombres Mexican Restaurant was known for the best margaritas in town, and she and her best friend, Patricia, tried to visit at least every other month.

"Any progress?"

"I'm now sixth on the list." The last time she'd checked, five months ago, she'd been tenth.

"Fantastic." Patricia raised her glass in a toast. "But Sam, even though you keep saying you want a baby, I still don't understand why you don't want to wait until you remarry."

Clinking their glasses together, they each drank. Then Sam said, "You know how I feel. Marriage is not in the cards for me. I'm not even dating, so it's not like remarriage is an issue. I'm thirty-one. I want a child. I can't wait too much longer."

Patricia winced. She and Sam were the same age.

"Hey, you have a boyfriend." Sam hurried to console her. "Who keeps begging you to marry him. You're the one who doesn't want to be tied down."

"Still, raising a child alone is tough."

"True. But I can do it, you know I can. Just because Eric and I divorced doesn't mean I have to give up on my dream of being a mother."

Patricia knew how badly Sam longed for family. "I agree, but Sam, not that much time has passed since your divorce. You might meet someone, try again."

"Even if I do, you know I can't conceive. The plane crash did something to me. They've already run all the tests." Sam snatched up another chip and dunked it in the dish of salsa. She wanted her friend to stop rehashing what couldn't be changed. "Can we drop this now? I *was* excited about the adoption agency's call."

"I'm sorry." Patricia looked anything but. "But let me say one more thing. I bet if you adopt, you'll turn up pregnant."

"You need a man for that."

"You're sixth on the list. By the time you get moved up to the number one spot, you might have a man."

Sam made a rude sound.

Doggedly, Patricia continued. "You know how celebrities are always adopting and then they get pregnant. Look at Brangelina."

"I'd rather not."

Wisely, Patricia dropped the topic. "Tell me what's really bothering you."

Biting her lip, Sam considered. Then, in a few words, she told about the sensations Luc Herrick aroused in her.

"Sam…" From the tone of Patricia's voice, something was worrying her. "I don't know about him. He makes me uneasy. He's been around the clinic a couple of times now, asking pointed questions about you healing that wolf pup. When I asked him what he knew about that, he just shrugged and said something to the effect that the wolf let itself out."

"He said the same thing to me." She took a deep breath. "You didn't tell him anything, did you?"

"Of course not. But he seemed more interested in what *you* could do than in learning about the werewolf."

"Can you blame him? Even if he's writing a book, he knows such a thing is impossible."

"Impossible?" Patricia widened her eyes in mock surprise. "But Charles Pentworth saw the werewolf, remember? So did several others. More than one person. Therefore, it must be true."

Back on familiar ground, Sam laughed. Teasing she could deal with. "Joining Charles's camp, are you?"

Her friend grinned back. "You never know."

"Yesterday Luc was trying to convince me that there are a lot of other species roaming around among us."

"Other species?" Patricia looked intrigued. "Like what?"

"Mermaids for one."

"Anatomically impossible."

"And vampires, ghosts, shape-shifters."

This time, Patricia didn't comment. Instead, she stabbed a bit of avocado with her fork and leaned forward. "You know, sometimes I wonder. You can heal animals by touching them. If you can do that, why do you refuse to believe a werewolf is possible? For someone who can practically perform miracles, you seem awfully close-minded sometimes."

Perform miracles. Sam had told Luc she was not a miracle worker. Putting the thought from her mind, she took another bite of her tortilla. "Close-minded works well for me."

Patricia shook her head. "If you're happy, I'm happy. But you need to be careful around this Luc guy."

"I will. I really think he's harmless."

"As long as he doesn't find out what you can do. I'm afraid he wants to use you. Though you could do an awful lot of good."

Sam sighed. That was another old discussion, and one that invariably led nowhere.

The waiter arrived with their second round. "Your dinners will be right out, ladies."

They both nodded, watching him walk away.

"My turn to change the subject." Taking a deep breath, Sam snagged another chip. "After this, do you want to go shopping with me?"

Patricia stared, her own chip halfway to her mouth. "Shopping? You don't like to shop."

"I know, but I want to decorate the nursery."

"The…do you mean that empty extra bedroom?"

"Yes. The nursery."

"You're sixth down the list. It could be months, maybe even a year or two, before they call with a baby for you."

With a shrug, Sam nodded. "True, but I still want to decorate. It might take me that long to get the room exactly like I want."

"You're scaring me." Patricia rolled her eyes. "What happened to the laid-back gal I know and love?"

"She's got an agenda now," Sam stated firmly, then waited. She knew her friend. Patricia adored shopping. She wouldn't be able to resist.

A second later, she tilted her head. "What exactly did you want to go shopping for, anyway?"

"Furniture. Since I have a dresser I'm refinishing, I want to buy a crib and changing table. And of course, the all-important rocking chair."

"Hmm." Patricia crossed her arms. "I suppose you haven't thought about maybe painting the room first?"

"I already did. Last weekend I painted all four walls yellow."

"Seriously?"

"Yes. I want to be ready when they call." Ever

since her application to adopt had been accepted, she'd hardly been able to think of anything else.

The waiter reappeared, carrying a large tray. "Here you go." He placed their plates in front of them, steaming platters of chicken enchiladas, rice and refried beans.

Everything smelled wonderful.

"And last but not least, flour tortillas. Do you ladies need anything else?"

Eyeing the food, they shook their heads, and he disappeared.

"I love this place." Sam closed her eyes, savoring the spicy flavors of cheese and chicken and cilantro. "It always smells so wonderful in here."

"You know, you're one of the only people I know who mentions scent before sight."

"Is that bad?"

"Of course not." Patricia looked thoughtful. "It's a trait peculiar to some animals, particularly canines."

They finished their meal and paid, then sauntered out into the bright sunlight.

"Your car or mine?"

Since Patricia drove a Dodge pickup, Sam chose it.

"More room to carry stuff," she explained. "Let's go look at cribs."

Several hours later, with their mission accomplished, they arrived back at Sam's house. She'd chosen a pale butterscotch for the nursery, a soothing color and one that would work for either a boy or a girl. For decorations she'd done forest scenes, huge cartoon animals romping joyfully among towering trees.

Helping her carry in the crib, Patricia stopped in amazement. "Wow. This looks fantastic. Did you use stencils?"

"Nope. I drew on the wall with pencil and then painted in the colors."

"I never knew you were an artist."

Sam shrugged. "I'm not. This was special."

They moved the crib into the corner she'd chosen and went back to the pickup for the matching changing table.

Patricia returned for the rocker and Sam wandered the nursery, running a hand over the furniture's smooth finish. Hard to imagine that one day there'd be a baby. Not just any baby, but hers. To love and protect and cherish. Her longing had become a palpable thing, keeping her awake at night.

Sam imagined herself pregnant. She pushed

away the thought. Rounds of fertility tests with abnormal results had convinced both her and Eric that she was sterile. She hadn't just lost her chance to have a baby; she'd lost a husband, too.

She turned toward the door as she heard Patricia coming back. Their friendship was one of the few good things left in her life. That, and Sam's unwavering ability to heal sick animals. A child to love would only enrich her and make her life complete.

Was that a *crib?* Having just pulled up to the curb in front of Sam's house, Luc sat in his rental car and watched her and Patricia carry a white-painted crib up the front sidewalk and into the house.

They emerged a few minutes later and did the same with what looked like a dresser or changing table. Lastly, Patricia came out alone and retrieved a matching wooden rocking chair. She locked her pickup and carried the chair into the house.

Now what? Luc scratched his head. All of the information he'd been given showed Samantha Warren as divorced. Unencumbered.

Was she pregnant? Who—and where—was the father?

Tamping down savage fury, Luc realized he

couldn't bear to think of her with another man. She was his mate, damn it. His.

He cursed. There he went with that insanity again. Hell hounds, he had it bad.

Desperate for distraction, he put in a call to Frank.

"Pregnant?" The mayor sounded as stunned as Luc. "How can that be? None of the data mentioned a boyfriend."

"None of the data mentioned she's pregnant, either. Looks like they're wrong on two points."

Frank didn't respond. Instead, he seemed in a hurry to get off the phone. "See what you can find out," he said. "Go talk to her. Do your thing. We have faith in you." He hung up.

We have faith in you. Closing his cell phone, Luc shook his head. Oddly enough, those words stung. How could anyone have faith in him when he had no faith in anything, least of all himself?

Nonetheless, even thinking of little Lucy in a hospital bed had him squaring his shoulders and getting out of the car. Though the test results had not yet been completed, he knew whatever was wrong with her was serious.

Since Patricia had left the front door wide-open, he didn't ring the bell. Patricia saw him first, eyes widening. "Sam," she called. "You have company."

A second later, Sam poked her head around a corner. She'd pulled her long hair into a ponytail and looked as fresh and youthful as a teenager.

While he stared, Patricia squinted at him as though he'd made a huge error in judgment.

"What are you doing here?" The vet's abrupt tone told him he wasn't welcome, at least by her. Luc didn't care. He wanted to talk to Sam, be with Sam. This all-consuming need had gotten so bad that he'd reached for her this morning, even though she'd never shared his bed.

She would. Soon.

He winced at the thought.

Obviously, Sam assumed he'd winced because of her friend's tone. "Welcome, Luc," she said softly, giving Patricia a warning look. "What can I do for you?"

The way she phrased her question had him again imagining all kinds of sensual delights. As color infused her face, he saw she shared his thoughts.

This made him absurdly happy, though he took care to hide his emotions from the two women.

"I came by to talk to you about these books." Pulling a card from his pocket, he scanned the list of titles he'd written down. Well aware that most of them were fairly rare texts and a library in a town the size of Anniversary would have to borrow them from someplace like Dallas, he'd planned to use them as an excuse to spend time with her.

Only to learn if she was a healer, of course.

"Let me see." Once he'd handed her the card, he smiled at Patricia, who still eyed him with distrust.

"Couldn't this have waited until the library is open in the morning?"

"Patricia!" Sam scolded. "Quit."

As his inner wolf bristled, recognizing the challenge, Luc chose to answer. "Yes, probably, but I knew getting some of these books will take time, and time is something I don't have in abundance."

They locked eyes. Patricia looked away first.

"What's the hurry?" she asked.

"I've got to go home soon. My best friend's daughter is seriously ill."

Both women stared. Then Sam's eyes grew soft. She moved closer, placing her hand on his arm. "I'm so sorry."

At the simple touch, he was lost. He forgot Patricia, forgot his supposed reason for visiting Sam's home, forgot everything but the woman looking at him with gentle doe eyes.

Crushing her to him, he claimed her mouth. The hunger that had been building in him since he'd

first seen her roared to life, like a starving wolf
released from a cage to hunt.

With reckless abandon, she returned his kiss,
her entire body quivering.

Loudly, Patricia cleared her throat. Once, twice,
then a third time.

Sam pushed away. Reluctantly, Luc let her go.

Her chest heaved as she struggled to regain her
composure. "Wow," she said softly, touching her
mouth with her fingers.

"What the hell was that?" Ever the protector,
Patricia moved between them, eyeing Luc as
though she wanted to punch him.

"Patricia!" Though breathless, Sam's voice
carried authority. "Enough. This is between me
and Luc."

"I see." Expression wounded, her friend moved
away. "Then I'll let myself out." At the entryway,
she turned and faced Sam once more. "Don't say
I didn't warn you."

Then she left.

Sam returned her attention to Luc. Wariness
and wonder warred in her eyes. "We need to
talk," she said.

"I agree." He let out a long, audible breath.

"Sit." Motioning to the sofa, she took a seat in

the overstuffed chair on the other side of the coffee table.

Though he didn't want to sit—he wanted to pace—he acceded to her wishes and lowered himself onto the edge of the soft cushions.

"Why did you do that?" Her cheeks still bloomed with color. "Kiss me, I mean."

Regarding her, he noted how she clasped and unclasped her hands. "Because I wanted to."

Evidently, his nonanswer gave her the courage to be blunt. "I don't do one-night stands."

"I'm not looking for a one-night stand."

She stared, a bemused look in her eyes. The very air between them felt electrified.

"What *are* you looking for then?" she asked, her voice soft.

"You."

Deeper color suffused her face, yet he knew from the little quirk at the corner of her lips that his answer had pleased her. Even if she had no idea what kind of beast he was, or even of her own shifter heritage, he knew she felt the invisible tie between them as strongly as he.

How could she not? Mates always did.

"Patricia says you want to use me."

Dangerous ground.

"Use you how?"

Instead of answering, she shook her head.

Knowing it was too soon, yet aware he had little time, Luc considered broaching the reason he'd traveled to Texas.

Instead, he asked about the crib.

"Oh, that." She bit her lip. "I'm trying to adopt a baby."

His first reaction was fierce joy that there wasn't another man. His second was astonishment. She couldn't have floored him more if she'd tried.

"Why?"

Pain darkened her eyes to a rich coffee color. "It's a long story."

He wanted to know everything about her. "If it's not too painful, I'd like to hear." His heart thumped three times in his chest while she decided. Then, with a small nod, she took a deep breath.

"My mother and I were on our way to a vacation in Mexico two years ago. We were on Flight 601." Pausing, she gazed at him as though she expected him to recognize what that meant.

An instant later, he did. "Was that the one that crashed on landing?"

She nodded.

"There were only, what, ten survivors?" He

couldn't believe she'd nearly… No. He couldn't even think such a thing. Not only would the Pack—and Lucy—have lost a healer, but he couldn't imagine a world without Sam in it.

"Yes, ten. I lived. My mother didn't." Sam's voice cracked. In awe, he watched her visibly regain control of herself and square her shoulders.

Still, she wouldn't look at him. She gazed at her hands, twisting them together in her lap.

"Anyway, I was injured in the crash. Though they aren't quite certain what caused this, it seems to have made me…infertile. Eric—my ex-husband—and I wanted children. When I couldn't have them, he found someone who could."

The magnitude of her loss astounded Luc. He'd lost his brother and suffered boundless guilt over his failure to save him. Yet Sam had not only lost her mother, she'd lost her husband and her dreams of a family.

Chest tight, Luc rose and went to her, kneeling beside her chair and pulling her close. He'd just met this woman, yet he felt as if he'd known her forever, and realized she was more damaged than he. Both inside and out. He didn't wonder at his reaction to her, finally accepting what his every instinct told him she was.

His mate.

Whether or not she could heal remained to be seen.

Inhaling the vanilla sent of her hair, he offered what little comfort he could, knowing it was not enough.

For an instant she let him hold her. Then, stiffening, she twisted out of his arms and to her feet.

"Don't." Her dark look full of pain, she strode away from him. Her agitated pacing reminded him of the Pack. Shifters and wolves both paced.

Sam was more shifter than she realized, even if she couldn't change.

A thought struck him. "Do you take any medicine for allergies?"

She stared at him as if she thought he'd gone insane.

"No. What does that have to do with anything?"

Lifting one shoulder in a shrug, he didn't answer, though inwardly he felt relief. One of the ingredients in allergy medications could subvert a shifter's ability—and need—to change. If that had been the case, and if Sam had been unconsciously blocking her basic need to shift, when she stopped taking the pills, she would know the truth about herself. She would have been able to become a wolf.

And she wouldn't have been able to heal.

His cell phone chirped, shrill in the quiet room. "Hello?"

"Luc?" It was Carson Turner, Luc's closest human friend. "I've got some bad news."

Something in Carson's voice... Luc felt a stab of fear deep in his gut.

"Tell me, how's the hunt for the healer coming?" Carson was clearly trying to compose himself enough to deliver his news.

Cautiously, Luc told him it was going okay.

"Okay isn't good enough. Lucy's very sick. We've finally found out what's wrong with her. The CT scan showed a large brain mass—" His voice cracked and he was unable to finish.

Luc couldn't believe his ears. "A brain mass? What does that mean? What is it?"

"Lucy has a brain tumor." Carson's voice broke again.

Closing his eyes against the wave of grief, Luc waited.

A moment later, Carson continued. "Medulloblastoma. Malignant. And worse, the tumor is inoperable. Even if it wasn't, even if they were able to cut it out and treat her with radiation and chemo, it'd probably come back."

Not Lucy! Luc could see her as she'd been only a short month ago, a giggling, happy child, overflowing with a boundless curiosity about life. "Then you're telling me...?"

Carson took a deep breath. "Buddy, these kinds of tumors are nearly always..." He couldn't go on, the word he hadn't said hanging between them.

Fatal.

"No." Luc refused to believe it. "Get a second opinion. Hell, get a third. There's got to be someone who can operate."

"I know. We are. We've got a call in to Sloan-Kettering in New York City. There's a pediatric oncologist there who is known for handling this kind of thing."

"What about the blood work?" Though he hated to, Luc had to ask. Halflings' blood was irregular enough to raise flags among the human medical community.

"Dr. Nettles is one of us," Carson said tiredly. "He's Pack. He'll take care of the little problem with the blood work. But I don't think any of the standard medical options are going to help too much longer. We need a miracle."

Tension coiled in Luc's gut. He knew exactly what his best friend wanted to say next.

On the other end of the phone line, Carson went silent. Luc knew him well enough to realize his friend was waiting for a response.

A miracle? He glanced at Sam. She had told him she wasn't a miracle worker.

"I still don't know anything, Carson," Luc told him quietly. "I need a bit more time."

"Time? We've run out. We can't wait any longer for the healer. Even if you're not a hundred percent certain, anything is better than doing nothing. You can't imagine how it feels to have to sit by and watch your little girl die."

Ah, but in a way Luc could well imagine. After all, Kyle had died a slow and painful death. "What do you want me to do?" he asked.

"Bring the healer here to help Lucy."

"I—" Luc's stomach clenched. "I don't know if she'll come. She knows nothing, Carson."

There was a moment of silence. Then Carson asked in a shocked voice, "You mean she's not aware she's a Halfling?"

"Correct."

"She doesn't know about the Pack?"

"No."

"That doesn't matter." Carson sounded firm— and desperate. "You've got to tell her. Don't you understand? Lucy won't live if you don't convince this healer to come."

"But…" Luc shot another glance at Sam, who was still silently watching and listening.

"Luc, they've given Lucy a month, max. Her doctor has said it's more a matter of weeks. Weeks! Please. If anyone can help save her life, you can. I have faith in you, Luc."

Luc swallowed, unable to reply for the ache in his throat. *Faith in him?* Again, the exact same words Frank had used.

Hell hounds.

"I'll do what I can," he said, despair making him finally relinquish his death grip on the phone. Closing it, he dropped back into the chair, head in his hands. Throat aching, he tried to make sense of it all.

As he'd suspected, Lucy wasn't merely seriously ill. She was dying. And fast.

He'd thought he'd have a bit more time. Worse, he'd let his attraction to Sam get in the way of what he'd come here to do. Find a healer. Help his people. And save a little girl from dying.

"Luc?" Sam's voice was tentative.

Dazed, Luc lifted his head. He could only stare at her, trying to comprehend her question. Feeling as if he were operating underwater, he pulled out his wallet and removed a photo, handing it to her. "This is Lucy. The child I told you about. She's my best friend's little girl, and he just told me she's dying."

Chapter 4

Reluctantly, Sam took the picture, hoping Luc didn't notice how her fingers trembled. Staring at the dark-haired toddler grinning up at the camera, she caught her breath. A familiar pain blossomed in her chest. By now she'd have thought she'd be used to it, that awful ache that reminded her she had no child of her own. Until the adoption came through—if it ever did—she guessed she'd have to live with the sense of loss.

Beloved child.

"She's beautiful," Sam said. "What's wrong with her?"

He swallowed, and she could see him fighting back tears. "She has a brain tumor. She's only three."

Sam handed the photo back, her heart aching for the little girl and her family. "What about surgery? Do they plan to remove the tumor?"

"No." His voice held a desperate kind of finality. "The doctors say it's inoperable. Even if they could operate, this one is malignant, which means it would come back."

Malignant. Inoperable. Bleak words, without hope. "What are her chances?"

"These kinds of tumors are nearly always fatal."

"*Nearly* always." Seizing the one hopeful thing in all he'd said, she watched him. "That means she has a chance, no matter how slim, right?"

"No. Carson—that's her dad—said they told him she has less than a month to live. Lucy is the reason I came here to Anniversary, Sam. To find someone who can help her."

"We're not known for our doctors. You'd have better luck in Dallas or Houston."

"I didn't come here for a doctor."

She blinked. "I don't understand."

"I know I promised not to ask you again without good reason, but the stakes have changed." He took a deep breath, his gaze sharp and assessing.

"I need to know the truth. Can you heal with your hands? Are you a healer?"

Even though he didn't say the words, she could hear the unspoken part of his plea. *Because if you are, you can save Lucy.*

But he was wrong. Even if she admitted to him what her hands could do, her gift only worked with animals. She knew that; once when Patricia had been sick, Sam had tried to heal her and failed.

"I…" She didn't know what to say. Though she felt horrible for the little girl—and him—admitting anything about her ability to heal animals wouldn't do any good.

"I'm sorry," she finally told him. "I can't help you."

Shaking his head, he moved closer, his mouth tight and grim. When he touched her shoulder, she wanted to lean into him. But she didn't—she couldn't. Not when she'd had to deny him the miracle cure he so actively sought.

"I'm sorry," she said again.

"Don't be. Sam, I know the truth. The wolf pup—Tomas—told me you healed him."

A soft gasp escaped her. She'd thought she'd imagined the wounded animal revealing his name. In all the years she'd been healing creatures, there had only been one other time when she'd thought the animal had attempted to directly communicate with her.

She didn't know what to say.

Wearing a humorless smile, he watched her. "He gave you his name, didn't he?"

Eyes wide, she didn't respond.

"Tomas said he was badly injured, dying maybe. He claims you laid your hands on him and he felt warmth, then rapid healing. He swore he could feel his wounds close, his bones knit back together. Is this true?"

Again she said nothing, balancing on the balls of her feet so she could flee at any second. Luc couldn't know. He couldn't.

"Please, Sam." Breathing her name, he cupped her chin, gently making her meet his gaze. "Tell me the truth. Can you heal?"

Animals, she cried out silently. *Not little girls.*

"Luc, I'm so sorry." Holding out her hands, she offered an apology. "I can't help your friend's child. That's the truth."

His expression anguished, Luc ignored her outstretched arms. He opened his mouth to speak, but closed it instead. Jerking his head in a terse nod, he pivoted and walked off, his stride both swift and awkward. He left without another word, closing the door firmly behind him.

Sam barely suppressed the urge to go after him. His departure felt like an ending, as painful as though she'd inadvertently closed another chapter of her life. One that promised the sun, moon and stars.

The little girl was dying. And as much as Luc— or she—might wish it, there was nothing she could do to help.

Why she felt so guilty, she didn't know. She hadn't lied, or even denied that she could heal. There'd been no reason for him to know she could help animals only, as he'd come to find a miracle cure for a dying three-year-old girl. Why he thought she could perform such a miracle, she didn't know.

Unless…no. Not possible. Despite the fact that the wolf pup had escaped from a closed cage and a locked clinic, she didn't believe in werewolves.

Yet how had he known the wolf pup's name? Even worse, how had she?

Feeling restless, she picked up her phone and called Patricia.

"Tired of making out with Romeo already?" her friend teased.

"Yes. No." Sam blew out her breath in a puff. "Let me tell you why he came over today."

After she'd relayed the story, Patricia whistled. "Now that's almost as bizarre as you both having the same name for that wolf. Did you maybe accidentally let that slip?"

"Absolutely not. Luc and I have barely discussed the wolf pup. As a matter of fact, the last time we did was when he asked me if I could heal. After that, he promised not to ask me again without justification."

"I'd say a little girl dying is plenty."

They both fell silent for a moment, contemplating.

"Sam, are you sure you couldn't help her?" Patricia asked hesitantly.

"You know my gift only works on animals."

"Yes, but things might have changed. I mean, I know you tried to heal me once, years ago, but maybe you've grown stronger since then."

"I doubt it."

"I know!" Patricia's tone lightened. "We can test it. All we need is a sick little kid."

"Right. And have the parents calling the police on me. No thanks."

"You owe it to this little girl to find out. Let me phone my sister. Maybe one of her brood has a cold or something and we can visit. That way you can try."

Sam sighed. Patricia got as tenacious as a bulldog when she had her mind set on something. "Fine. Call me back."

While Sam waited, she paced. She kept seeing the little girl in the picture, so happy and carefree. Sam didn't like to imagine her motionless in a hospital bed, with tubes running from her to machines. Even worse, Sam's mind kept replaying Luc's anguished expression over and over, until she thought she'd go insane.

She'd known him for only a couple of days. Why did he have such a profound effect on her?

Two minutes later, the phone rang.

"It's a go," Patricia said. "I'll swing by to pick you up and we'll head out there. Oh, you had the chicken pox when you were eight, the same time I did, right?"

"Yes."

"Then let's see if you can heal Tory. She's the six-year-old hoyden."

Sam couldn't believe they were actually going to go through with this. She replaced the receiver and went to the front porch to wait, watching as the sun set in a pearly, pink glow. If her gift worked with Patricia's niece, they'd have some explaining to do, but at least she'd know for sure.

Maybe then she could put an end to her unreasonable guilt over failing to help Luc and the adorable little girl.

Though he could not smell her scent, he knew she was there. For the second week he watched from the fringe of trees at the edge of the backyard.

Impatience clawed at him, like a rabbit trying to escape his jaws. Again he wondered—should he enter while Samantha was gone? The urge to touch her, to and try and get closer, as if that alone could tell him if she had the power, was strong.

But no, she didn't know him, though they shared a past. She would not remember, nor care. The bitterness of that knowledge ate like acid in his stomach.

Still, Samantha was his. Tied by blood. His to do with as he pleased. If she could help him now, then the years of self-doubt and envy would be well worth the delay.

For now, he would continue to wait and see. Watch and learn if the gift truly resided in her hands. Only once he knew the truth would he know if he could use her for his own gain.

The gift that kept on giving.

Laughing quietly at his own joke, he blended back into the shadows, slipping away to wait and watch.

* * *

As the sun traveled toward the horizon, Luc headed into town for supplies. Though traffic was light, he rounded a curve and came to a sudden halt as the pickup in front of him did the same. Several cars had pulled over on the side of the road and people were clustered around something, a small, motionless shape on the pavement.

The pickup in front of Luc exited the line of traffic and pulled over.

Obeying his instincts, Luc did as well.

Joining the small crowd, he saw they were all staring at a cat, so motionless and still it might have been dead. On the edge of the group, a teenage girl clutched her friend and cried in noisy, gasping gulps.

"What happened?" Luc asked quietly.

"I didn't mean to hit him." The girl spoke so fast her words ran together. "He came out of nowhere and…the sun was in my face, and…" She resumed her sobbing.

Kneeling, Luc inspected the small animal. Except for the blood, if he'd come across the cat anywhere else, he'd have believed it only slept.

"Is he dead?" one of the women asked.

"There's no movement, no breathing that I can

see." Yet he sensed the animal's life force, stubbornly remaining inside the cat's body.

He held his finger up, touching it to the nose. An almost imperceptible response told him he'd been right.

"He's still alive."

Immediately, the teenager stopped crying, turning tearstained and reddened cheeks to him. "We've got to get him to the vet."

"I'll do it," Luc said. No one questioned his authoritative tone. "I've got to be careful how I lift him—he might have internal injuries."

Removing his shirt, despite two older women's wide-eyed reaction, he stated, "I'm going to put this down and someone can help me lift him onto it. We'll use the shirt like a stretcher." Luckily he had a spare T-shirt in the backseat.

The teenager stepped forward. "Let me do it. I'm the one who hit him."

Once the still-unconscious cat had been placed on the backseat, Luc sped to Patricia's veterinary clinic. The parking lot was empty save for a few employees' cars. Patricia's pickup wasn't in her regular spot.

The receptionist looked up as he pushed through the door. "Can I help you?"

"I have an emergency. Can you call Patricia—Dr. Lelane? Please?" In a few words, he explained the urgent situation and his rush to save the small animal, which was still unconscious in the back of his car.

The receptionist picked up the phone and dialed. Speaking softly for a moment, she eventually nodded and replaced the receiver. "She's on her way," she said.

"I'll be out by my vehicle. I'm afraid to move the cat." At her nod, he went outside to wait.

The phone rang one more time. Watching for Patricia, Sam considered letting the call go to her answering machine, but at the last minute she sprinted for the kitchen and grabbed the receiver.

"Sam, I'm sorry." It was Patricia, sounding frustrated. "We'll have to do the test another time. I've got a wounded cat that was hit by a car waiting for me at the clinic. Katie says he is in pretty bad shape. Some man brought him in. Can you meet me there, just in case?"

"Sure. Make certain the back door is unlocked."

"I will. See you in a few minutes."

Luc prowled around outside his car, the unconscious cat inside. Though he hadn't smelled death when he handled the feline, he knew in some cases passing away would be more merciful.

He had a sad feeling this might be one of those. The wolf in him wanted to celebrate life, to run free. Ruthlessly, he squashed the urge to change.

Patricia's pickup pulled into the parking lot. Luc waved, pointing at his car.

She parked in her usual spot. A moment later, head up, an angry look glinting in her eyes, she strode toward him. "I can't believe you ran over a cat."

"I didn't." Briefly, he explained what had happened.

Her expression softened. "Where is it?"

He opened the back door. "I used my shirt as a makeshift stretcher."

"Excellent. Help me get it inside."

Grasping one side, he waited until Patricia had taken the other. Moving slowly, they carried the animal in, going down a long hallway to an examining room.

"Put it down here. Gently, gently."

Once he'd done as she asked, Patricia gave Luc a quick once-over before turning her attention back to the wounded animal. "Thanks. I'll take it from here."

"Are you going to have to euthanize it?"

Distracted, she didn't look up. "I don't know. I've got to see how badly he's hurt."

Luc didn't move. "You know as well as I do that he has internal injuries."

"There's no way to tell that for sure without an X-ray." The vet's tone was brusque, the look she gave him sharp.

Suddenly, he realized what she meant to do. He knew as instinctively as the distraught teenager who'd hit the cat that the feline was beyond saving. The fact that he'd lived this long with no doubt massive internal injuries was a good sign, but he read the truth in Patricia's carefully averted face.

The cat would die unless a miracle occurred. And Patricia just happened to have access to her own private source of miracles.

She was going to call in Sam to heal the cat.

If she did and the animal lived, he'd know without a doubt Sam had lied to him. The thought was bitter.

"I'll wait." Crossing his arms, he leaned against the wall.

"Why?" Though she acted professional, Luc read the hostility in Patricia's tone. "This isn't even your cat."

"I love cats," he lied. At best, felines and shifters

existed with an uneasy truce. "Since I brought him in, I feel a personal interest in his welfare. I want to make sure he's all right."

Patricia sighed. "All right, but you'll need to take a seat out in the waiting room. I'll keep you apprised of the cat's prognosis."

He did as she asked, though instead of sitting, he chose to stand in front of the large window. From here he could see not only the parking lot, but also the street heading east and west. When Sam's car pulled in, he'd know it.

Barely ten minutes later, he spotted her blue compact. She swung into a parking spot beside Patricia's truck. Heart pounding, Luc watched as she got out and hurried around to the back of the building. As he'd suspected she would.

Drumming his fingers on the window, he knew he had to figure out a way to get back there and see what happened for himself.

"Excuse me, sir?"

Turning, he saw the veterinary assistant had come from the back. "I'm terribly sorry, but Dr. Lelane has asked me to let you know the cat you brought in didn't make it."

"What?" He stared. On the verge of demanding proof, he grudgingly realized Sam could have arrived too late. Still, something about this didn't feel quite right.

"The cat is dead," she reiterated gently. "I'm sorry."

"May I see him?"

The young woman frowned. "Excuse me?"

"May I see the cat?"

She looked away. "No, I'm sorry, sir. The doctor will take care of disposing of him." Starting to hurry away, she apparently remembered something at the last moment and turned. "Oh, and Dr. Lelane said she'd cover the cost. You don't have to worry about paying anything." With that, she vanished into the back room.

He thought about following her, but didn't. Walking out to the parking lot, instead of going to his rental car, he went around to the back door. Trying the handle, he found it locked. Sam must have locked it after her.

Two could play this game. Because of Lucy, he had to know. He would wait and confront Sam when she came out. If she had been able to perform any miracles, he figured he'd be able to tell, somehow.

If there was even the smallest possibility that Sam was a healer, he had to get her to New York in time to prevent Lucy's death.

Stepping into the shadow of a huge pecan tree, Luc settled down to wait.

Locking the back door behind her, Sam hurried to the operating room. On the table lay a huge gray cat, barely breathing.

"Is he…?"

"Not yet. He's severely injured. There's nothing else I can do for him. He's dying." Urgency made Patricia's tone clipped. "Touch him."

Taking a deep breath, Sam moved forward. Laying her hands lightly on the wounded animal, she glanced at her friend. From just this, a whisper-soft touch, she could feel the cat's weakened life force trying to slip away.

Something inside her flared. Connected. Burned its way through her fingers into the feline and tugged on the animal's damaged spirit.

While she wasn't entirely sure how this healing gift of hers worked, she knew the energy flowed from the inside out, helping the animal heal itself.

Patricia stroked the cat's head, respectfully silent. She knew once the healing process started, it couldn't be interrupted.

The animal made a sound, a cross between a

moan and a whimper. Echoes of pain radiated from feline to woman, making Sam flinch.

Heal.

Concentrating, she closed her eyes. Her hands sizzled, unbearably hot, but she bore the burning with only the barest hitch in her breath.

The cat whimpered again.

Pain, so much pain. He'd been chasing a squirrel, gaining on the rodent, when the car had come out of nowhere. The cat knew to avoid the motorized monster, but intent on his prey, he'd never had a chance. Sam saw images of metal and panic, teeth and claws and blood—exploding in agony.

Heart pounding in her chest, she kept her hands in place. *Heal.* Her entire body vibrated, like a hummingbird yearning for nectar, and she tasted the faint metallic tang of blood as she bit her tongue.

The cat moaned, still unconscious, writhing in pain. Inside, Sam stifled an answering groan. As she melded with him, they thought as one. She felt what he did, and vice versa. How or why this happened, she dared not question, for fear of destroying the gift.

Gradually, the feline went still. His breathing steadied, heartbeat normal and strong. Finally, he slept, pain free.

All at once, the heat left her palms, and her spirit disconnected. Done.

"There." Opening her eyes, Sam removed her hands from the cat's fur and took a deep, shuddering breath. "He's all better."

"Girl, if we do find out your gift works on people…" Patricia clapped her on the shoulder. "Thank you so much. Now go home, go to bed. I know what healing does to you. You look exhausted."

"I am." Sam searched her friend's freckled face. "What will happen to him now?"

"I'll try to find someone to take him. I'll make some calls. If he's missing, we'll find his owners. If not, surely someone will give a young cat like this a home."

"I want him." Sam spoke without hesitation, knowing bone-deep that this was the right thing for her.

Patricia's mouth fell open. "You want him? Why? You've never had a pet."

"I know." Sam laughed at Patricia's amazement. "But I think it's time. He can be my watch-cat."

Shaking her head, her friend grinned. "Fine. If no one comes forward to claim him, since you healed him, he's yours."

"Good." Sam took a step back and nearly fell.

"I need to get home." Her voice sounded guttural, low and exhausted.

"You look horrible," Patricia exclaimed. "I keep a cot in the storeroom. Would you like to lie down on that?"

"No." Sam closed her eyes and felt the room move. Swaying, she opened them again and grabbed for the counter. "I'd rather go home."

"I don't think you should drive."

Raising her head, Sam blinked against the dizziness. "You're probably right. Can you take a moment and run me home?"

"Sure." Patricia drew her hand over the cat's silky fur. "But we'll need to take this guy with us. Luc Herrick brought him in and was asking a lot of questions."

Sam looked down, biting her lip, unable to keep from swaying on her feet.

"You need to sit down," Patricia said in a firm voice. "Rest a minute and then we'll get you and the cat out to my truck."

Pushing Sam gently onto her examination stool, she turned and carefully examined the still-unconscious animal. Then she gathered him in her arms. "Good as new."

Sam gave her friend a weak smile as Patricia

helped her up in turn and herded her toward the door. "Once you and this kitty are settled comfortably in the truck, I'll need to come back and let my receptionist know I'm out for an hour or so."

"What about your appointments?" Sam protested weakly.

"The clinic is closed," Patricia said. "My next one isn't scheduled until tomorrow morning."

Healing mustn't take long. Luc had barely stepped behind the tree when Sam and Patricia emerged from the back door. He dug his car key from his pocket, watching as they hurried for Patricia's pickup.

Sam stumbled, grabbing on to the nearest vehicle to keep from falling. Instinctively, Luc moved to help her.

But Patricia was closer. She pushed the unlock button on her remote. Luc slipped back into the shadows behind the tree.

She had something in her arms. Squinting, he tried to make out the lumpy shape the vet carried.

Once Sam had climbed into the truck, Patricia carefully handed over the bundle. Suddenly, Luc realized what it was.

The cat.

The very same one he'd been told had died.

Now what? He started forward, then stopped. If he confronted her now, he might as well call her a liar.

Though, if she'd healed the cat, she hadn't exactly been truthful.

His stomach turned. *I'm no miracle worker,* she'd said. But if she'd healed this dying feline, she'd done exactly that. Performed a miracle. What kind of person could refuse to help a dying child? What kind of woman was his mate?

Watching them pull from the parking lot, he headed for his own car.

Time to find out.

Chapter 5

Once Sam buckled her seat belt, Patricia placed the still-unconscious cat on her lap before going around to the driver's side and climbing in. She didn't speak as she started the pickup and backed from the lot.

Stroking the cat's soft fur, Sam felt the animal purr. Though normally she didn't consider herself a cat person, she felt a special connection to this one. Healing often did that to her.

Patricia turned the radio to a classical music station, knowing this usually helped Sam sleep.

Sam gave her friend a grateful smile and let herself sink back into the leather seat. Once they reached the main road, she tried to keep her eyes open. Something worried her, an ethereal wisp of energy she'd seen or felt, though try as she might, she couldn't put her finger on what it was.

Eventually, the music and the motion and the exhaustion got to her, and she abandoned the fight to stay awake. Resting her head back, she let herself drift off.

"We're here." Patricia gently shook her shoulder. "Wait a minute and I'll come around and get the cat."

Managing a groggy nod, Sam sat up and flexed her shoulders, trying to wake up. If she could make herself move, it would be enough to keep her from slipping back into sleep. At least until she got to her bed. Then she'd give herself over to oblivion.

The sound of tires on gravel made her look up wearily. A car barreled down the long driveway, dust clouds obscuring the make and color.

"Uh-oh," Patricia muttered. "Look's like we've got company." She swore. "It's Luc Herrick. He's the one who brought the cat in today. I, uh, had my assistant tell him it died. You'd better let me handle him."

Luc? Weakly, Sam lifted her head and peered out the window. Even exhausted, she found the thought of seeing him gave her a jolt of energy.

As though he felt this, the animal in her arms stirred and let out a weak meow. The cat! Since Luc had brought him in, he'd know the now-healed feline had been near death. He'd be able to substantiate his claim that she could heal animals with a touch. And, judging by his emotional reaction to little Lucy's illness, he'd never believe Sam couldn't heal a child.

"Great," she groaned. "Just what I don't need."

"Stay put." Patricia got out, her low-heeled boots crunching on the gravel as she strode over to Luc's car. "What is it this time?" she asked. Sam could well imagine her friend, arms crossed, facing down the tall New Yorker. "Did you bring me another animal you just happened to witness being run over?"

"I'd like to talk to Sam for a moment." Luc's voice, firm and implacable as he refused to take the bait, sent shivers up Sam's spine. He sounded like whiskey and honey. Both potent and smooth.

He didn't seem to affect Patricia the same way. She sounded as though she might attempt to inflict bodily injury. "You'll have to come back later. She's not well."

Crap. Sam had to do something before this got

completely out of hand. Maybe if she went over there and talked to him, he'd leave.

After placing the still-groggy cat on the driver's seat, she got out of the truck. She took one step and the world tilted crazily. Staggering, she was glad she wasn't carrying the animal. Even empty-armed, she'd be lucky to avoid doing a face plant in the gravel. She prayed Luc didn't walk over to Patricia's truck.

"Sam!" Patricia's voice seemed to come from a distance. Weaving, Sam fell to her knees. She managed to throw out her hands in front of her, but couldn't stifle a sharp yelp as the gravel stung her knees and palms.

"Let me help you." Luc knelt down beside her. She could swear, even in her weakened condition, that she could smell his scent. Musk and lime, with a hint of fern-shaded forest.

"Are you all right?"

His touch felt far too good. She fought the urge to lean into him.

"Leave her alone." Patricia's emphatic voice vibrated with indignation, making Sam smile despite her bone-deep weariness.

Ah, but Sam didn't want him to leave her alone. The longer he held her, the better she felt.

Bemused, she finally gave in and leaned against him, breathing in his scent, savoring the feel of his sturdy body. How was this possible? The more they shared contact, the stronger she felt, as though his energy infused her.

Finally, she gathered enough strength to stand—but only with his help.

"Are you all right?" he murmured into her hair.

A shiver ran through her. Suddenly tongue-tied, she nodded. Tilting her head to look at him, she found him gazing at her with tenderness in his eyes.

Her heart turned over.

"How is the cat?" he asked quietly.

"He's resting."

"Really?" he drawled, looking from Sam to Patricia. "That's odd, since I was told the cat died."

"My assistant was mistaken," Patricia stated.

One look at Luc's implacable expression and Sam knew he didn't buy it. "Is he in your truck? I'd like to see him. You know, ever since I brought him in today, I've been worried about his health. But, since I was told he was dead, imagine my astonishment when I saw you carrying him out of the clinic and loading him into your truck."

"Leave the cat alone." Patricia moved to block him. "Look, he's still unconscious. On top of that,

Sam's really sick, as you can see. I've got to get both of them into the house so they can rest."

Keeping his arms around Sam, Luc shook his head. "I'd like to talk to Sam. Alone, if you don't mind."

Patricia shifted her weight from one foot to the other. "This is getting annoying."

"It's all right." Sam closed her eyes for a second, savoring Luc's strength. "We can talk."

Lips pressed together mutinously, Patricia glared at Luc. "I want both Sam and the cat in the house first." She led the way to the front door, yanking it open so Samantha and Luc could pass through. "Sam, you need to sit before you fall over."

Though she felt better, Sam sank down on the sofa.

Patricia went out to retrieve the cat. Holding him in her arms when she returned a minute later, she glared at Luc. "You wanted to see him. Here he is." Gently placing the animal on the soft couch cushion, she motioned him over.

After a cursory examination, during which the cat opened his eyes and sniffed at him, Luc glanced from Patricia to Sam. The intensity of his gaze would have melted steel. "We still need to talk. Alone."

"Sam?" Patricia crossed her arms again.

"It's all right," she sighed, longing foolishly for Luc to touch her once more. "It's late and you need to grab something to eat and get some rest. Luc is seeing things that don't exist. Either way, I can spare a few minutes."

"No more than a couple." Patricia's fierce tone dared him to argue. "You need to rest, too."

"Of course she does." He lowered himself to the sofa next to Sam, his jean-covered thigh touching hers.

All she could think was *Ahhh*. She closed her eyes, savoring the strength even this slight contact brought her. Her entire body vibrated at the tendrils of awareness she felt. No, more than that—need, desire, a sexual craving. For him.

Though she knew she should move away, she instead slid closer, snuggling against him and resting her head on his shoulder. She didn't dare look either at him or at her best friend, afraid of what her eyes might reveal.

Openmouthed, Patricia stared. Then, muttering under her breath, she headed for the door.

A moment passed. Sam waited for Luc to speak, bracing herself, desperately trying to formulate reasonable answers to the questions that were sure to come.

Instead, he got up from the couch. She shivered, feeling the absence of his body like a sharp ache. Rather than abating, her need flared, as though intensified by the end of contact. This shocked her, as did her suddenly high energy and sense of well-being. Healing always depleted her. Always. Until now.

Now, simply because he'd touched her... It was as if he, this stranger, could somehow replenish her.

Luc began pacing. She couldn't look away from his dark, masculine beauty. "I asked you for the truth, Sam," he said.

"I gave you the truth. I can't help your friend's little girl."

He shot her a cold smile edged with mockery. "First the wolf cub, now this cat. You lied to me. Me, your—" He broke off, the stark hurt in his eyes belying his scornful expression.

"Your what?" Confused, she sensed hidden layers to his words.

As he opened his mouth to speak, the front door slammed open. Patricia burst back inside.

"Don't you ever knock?" Luc drawled.

She ignored him, looking at Sam. "You're not going to believe this. As I was driving home, my cell phone rang. Mrs. Atkinson's poodle is missing. She's frantic. She's even called 911."

Sam sighed. She knew what that meant. "It's dark and you look exhausted. Have you even made it anywhere to grab a sandwich?"

"No. I was on my way when your friend here showed up with that cat. Now this."

"It's too dark."

"Try telling that to Mrs. Atkinson."

"Who's organizing the search?"

"Guess." Patricia's worry showed in the fine lines around her mouth. "Since Mrs. Atkinson brings that dog to see me at least every other week, she thinks I'm her best friend. She asked me to do it."

"And you couldn't turn her down."

"No." One of Patricia's weaknesses was that she couldn't say no to anything involving animals. Sam also found that to be one of her friend's most admirable qualities.

"I'll come help."

"I don't know if that's such a good idea." Patricia rubbed the back of her neck, managing to glare at Luc and smile at Sam almost at the same time. "In fact, it's a downright bad idea. You need to go to bed and sleep." She shot Luc another pointed look. "Otherwise, you'll collapse. You know how you are."

"What do you mean by that?" Luc asked.

Red slowly crept up Patricia's neck to her face. "Never mind. Sam's sick. She needs her rest."

"Actually, I feel amazingly better." And she did. Sam wasn't sure what to make of it, but she'd never had this much energy after a healing. Ever.

Patricia sighed. Knowing her as well as she did, she realized if Sam set her mind to do something, there'd be no stopping her. "Charles Pentworth and John Stobie have made Mrs. Atkinson hysterical. Both of them are claiming the werewolf has the dog. Mrs. Atkinson won't stop crying. I've called Dr. Ross to come and give her a sedative."

"Where are we meeting?" Sam lifted her chin, daring her friend to argue.

"The park. At least it's well lit. But someone said they saw the poodle heading into the woods."

The woods in the dark. Great. "I'll meet you there." Pushing herself up, Sam found Luc blocking her way.

"*We'll* meet you there," he said. "Give us ten minutes."

"Fine." Patricia sighed, shaking her hair loose from her ponytail and then gathering it up again. "I'll see you in a little bit. Since I'm recruiting volunteers, I've got a few more people to talk to first,

so wait for me if I'm a little late. Ten minutes."
With a tired wave, she left.

"I'll drive," Luc said when Sam emerged from
the bathroom. Despite the way her exhaustion kept
flickering back, then vanishing, she needed to
drive her own car, in case she needed to escape.

When they arrived at the park, she was sur-
prised at the size of the crowd despite the late hour.
Nearly every space in the lot had been taken, and
Luc had to park way in back.

As he and Sam walked across the well-lit con-
crete, they saw people milling in the children's play
area and near the start of the paths, small groups
clustered together and talking quietly. Everyone had
been issued a whistle to hang around their neck.

An awful, high-pitched shriek cut through the
murmur of small talk. From a tight knot of people
close to the gazebo, Mrs. Atkinson wailed again,
flailing her flabby arms. "My poor baby!"

After a moment of awkward silence, the
chatter resumed.

Someone blew a whistle. Immediately, the
crowd quieted. Patricia stepped up on the gazebo
steps and waved her bright orange bullhorn. Sam
saw she'd taken the time to freshen her makeup,
and was making an effort to appear energetic,

despite the fact that it was nearly 10:00 p.m. and she'd been up seventeen hours.

Patricia blew the whistle again to get everyone's attention.

"Listen up, people," she yelled, the bullhorn distorting as well as amplifying her voice. "Break up into groups of two or three and head into the woods. If you find the poodle, blow on your whistle, three sharp blasts." She demonstrated. "If he's injured, blow twice. I've got a portable vet kit here, just in case."

At those words, Mrs. Atkinson began to wail again. Patricia raised her bullhorn once more. "Now go. Make sure you have your flashlights. And call me the second you find anything. Anything at all. Tubby was last seen heading toward the lake."

"Tubby?" Luc raised an elegant brow. "Who names their poodle Tubby?"

"Little old ladies who feed a lot of table scraps." Despite herself, Sam laughed. "Every dog she's ever had has grown enormously fat. She had a Chihuahua when I was younger. That dog was enormous. He weighed twenty-one pounds and looked like a sausage with legs."

"Okay, so we're looking for an obese poodle?"

"Not that fat, not yet." Sam started walking toward the darkness. "Tubby's just very stocky. His name fits, actually."

Clicking his flashlight on, Luc kept pace with her. "I guess we're our own group of two."

A shiver ran down her spine. She ignored it. "I guess so." She wished she could stop thinking about that damn kiss.

Pushing aside a branch, she headed into the trees, far from the well-traveled hiking path. On both sides of them, flashlights showed that other groups were also entering the woods, fanning out so that every square inch would be covered.

"This is as thorough as searching for a child," Luc commented. "I'm surprised at the turnout, especially since it's after ten."

"Yeah, well, nothing much happens here in Anniversary. Something like this makes an event." Releasing a branch too early, she narrowly missed snapping it in his face. "I'm sorry. You know, this might be a bit rough going." She hoped she wasn't being too obvious, but she wanted him to leave before he pursued his earlier line of questioning.

Raising a brow, he smiled. "I can handle it, believe me."

"Maybe you can." She pointed her flashlight at

his feet. "But those expensive Italian loafers might not fare as well."

"If they don't, I'll buy another pair," he said calmly. "How did you know they were Italian?"

"They look it. Shoes are my one addiction. Well, shoes and tortilla chips with salsa," she amended.

The two of them beat the bushes for what felt like hours, going over every inch of underbrush with their flashlights. The energy humming between them was strangely exhilarating, banishing even the faint tendrils of exhaustion that had been threatening earlier.

Stepping out of the woods at the muddy lake-shore, Sam shone her beam at the water lapping the shore. "No Tubby. If he went down to the lake, he didn't go this way."

"Shhh." Luc's touch on her arm made her want to lean into him and purr. "Listen. I hear something. It's coming from that direction." He pointed toward a grove of trees.

Cocking her head, she strained her ears. "I don't—"

"Hush. That's a small dog whimpering." Luc started forward. "I think the poodle is over there. I can smell his fear and…pain. He's still alive, but badly hurt."

"Smell his...? What?"

Luc didn't answer, striding toward the area he'd pointed to.

As she hurried to keep up, a sense of unreality struck her. The cool, silver moonlight illuminated the hollows in his handsome, rugged face. He was beautiful and mysterious. Dangerous to her, but with the potential to become her savior.

Here, now, this place and time... This man... Sometimes she felt as if he knew all of her secrets instinctively. Every thought, every wish, every desire, right down to the bare bones of her soul.

But she'd only met him a little over two weeks ago.

Sam shook her head. Odd ideas, especially for her. She wasn't the slightest bit whimsical, nor given to flights of fancy. Except when Luc touched her. Or kissed her. At the memory, she felt a flash of heat. Taking a deep breath, she blinked to return to reality.

"Listen," he whispered.

Again she tried. This time, she heard faint cries, an animal's low wails of pain, and wondered how Luc had heard them from so far away.

Together, they hurried forward, flashlight beams in tandem, pushing aside the tangled brush.

In a small clearing, they found Tubby, immobile and caught in a vicious looking trap. His fine-boned leg looked to be shattered and his panting seemed shallow. Too shallow.

Sam wanted to weep. "I'd like to find whoever put this trap here and shut their foot in it so they can see how it feels."

Hearing her voice, the poodle slowly moved his head, gazing up at her with glazed eyes. Confused, he struggled to get to his feet to greet them. Instead, he thrashed once and gave a sharp yelp. Dried blood matted his white fur, and the leaves under him were all rust-colored.

He smelled of decay and death. Or, as Luc had said, of fear and pain.

"Not good," Luc grunted.

She looked up to find that, instead of watching the dog, he was studying her.

"He's lost a lot of blood," Sam agreed. Her fingers itched to touch the little dog and heal him. But she'd just healed the cat earlier that day. Once, several years ago, she'd attempted to heal two animals a day apart. The effort had nearly killed her. She'd been unconscious for twenty-seven hours, and Patricia had been on the verge of calling the hospital.

No, this time Sam couldn't help the poodle. Patricia would be on her own, with her veterinary skills and prayers. "Can you get him free?"

"Yes." Crouching down beside the dog, Luc examined the trap.

"Let me hold him." She moved closer. "He's out of his head with pain. I'm afraid he'll snap at you."

"Don't worry about that." As Luc knelt beside the animal, the dog ceased whimpering. Weakly lifting his head, Tubby sniffed at him. Then, to Sam's astonishment, he laid his little head on Luc's knee and sighed, closing his eyes.

Sam's throat ached. Tubby's actions were tantamount to a declaration of trust. Moved, she went around to the other side. "How can I help?"

"Wait until I get him free." Wincing, Luc pried apart the rusted metal and gently freed the poodle's mangled leg.

The injury didn't look good. Without her healing powers, the dog might have to endure an amputation, Sam knew. Only Patricia could say for sure.

"We need to blow the whistle," Luc stated. "The trap nearly severed his leg." When Luc gazed directly at her, Sam saw a question in his eyes. "Can you help him?"

The darkness suddenly felt suffocating.

She shook her head. "No."

"If you can heal this little dog, you must."

Chest tight, she stared at him, unable to speak. In a way, he was so right. And also so, so wrong.

How could she even think of making the attempt, when she knew what such an effort would cost her? Yet if she did nothing...

"Tubby will die if you don't." The urgency in his tone told her he spoke the truth. At that moment, the dog moaned. "At least do something to ease his pain."

She bit her lip. Luc didn't understand how standing by and doing nothing while Mrs. Atkinson's beloved pet suffered and died a slow death would hurt her.

But Sam knew if she tried, she'd only fail.

Patricia was the dog's only hope now.

Standing, Sam blew her whistle—two short blasts, then again. Patricia would know how to help Tubby.

"What are you doing?" Luc's quiet voice matched his expressionless face. Only his eyes registered emotion. In them, she saw both sorrow and anger.

"I'm calling Patricia. If anyone can help Tubby, she can." Kneeling down beside the dog, Sam murmured words of encouragement, taking care not to place her hands on the animal's bloodstained coat. She couldn't afford to risk even an accidental transfer of energy.

As Luc started to argue, Patricia burst into the clearing, carrying a large lantern. Two of her employees flanked her, one lugging a large ice chest on wheels, the other holding a plastic board to use as a portable stretcher, as well as another lantern.

"You found him?"

"Yes. He's hurt."

"How badly?"

Jaw working, Luc stepped aside so that she could see.

Patricia gave a horrified gasp, dropping to her knees beside Sam. Tubby moaned again. The vet smoothed back enough fur so she could feel the animal's skin. "He's burning up. His heartbeat is uneven, unsteady."

"Can you give him something for the pain?" Sam kept her attention focused on the dog, avoiding looking at Luc.

"Yes." She readied a syringe.

Sides heaving, Tubby began to shiver convulsively.

"He's in shock." Patricia turned her sharp gaze on Sam. Sam cut her eyes to Luc, then gave the tiniest shake of her head. Patricia knew she couldn't heal two animals this close together.

"Can you help him?" Luc asked.

"I don't know." Grimly, Patricia motioned to one of her assistants to bring the ice chest. "But I'm sure as hell going to try."

Swallowing past the lump in her throat, Sam whispered words of encouragement to the poodle. She didn't know if the dog could hear her, but she hoped she was helping in some small way.

"You all need to leave," Patricia ordered. "Sam will stay and assist me. Go back and tell the others that Tubby's been found. Don't tell Mrs. Atkinson how badly he's hurt."

The two teenage vet assistants exchanged looks, then took off at a jog. They left both the portable stretcher and the ice chest.

Eyes narrowed, Luc looked from Sam to Patricia and back again. He didn't budge. "I'm not going anywhere."

Pushing herself to her feet, Patricia stood toe to toe with him, her nose inches from his. "Do you want the dog to die?"

Amazed, Sam watched as Luc bared his teeth. He appeared to realize what he was doing, and shook his head instead. "Of course not."

"Then go. Now." Her fierce tone left no room for argument.

"Please," Sam added. She didn't look at Luc, nor watch for other searchers. Instead, knowing what she had to do despite the danger to herself, she let her awareness of everything except the wounded dog fade.

Dimly, she registered the sound of leaves crunching under Luc's shoes as he moved away. Then she placed her hands gently on Tubby's heaving sides.

"Sam?" Patricia's voice came from a long way off. "What are you doing? You know better than to try and heal now. You know you can't—"

Sam tuned her out. The heat in her hands began to build. Images—of the moist earth, soft beneath Tubby's feet. A smorgasbord of scents, rabbit scat and birds and the occasional rodent.

Then...*snap*. The clang of the trap snapping shut, Tubby's surprised yelp, the awful hurt. Clawing at a nonliving enemy, not understanding the attacker. Then blackness. The poodle had gone limp, unconscious, howling only inside at the agonizing pain.

Sam's heart pounded, her blood pulsing through her veins. Energy rushed through her, making her skin and fingers burn.

Heal.

Even as she thought this, Tubby's bones began to knit together. The bleeding stopped, the wound closed, skin formed, fur recovered. Tubby stopped shivering and lay motionless, his breathing less labored.

Finally, as her heartbeat slowed and exhaustion overtook her, Sam knew Tubby was once again whole. Healed.

Utterly depleted, she lifted her head and tried to make out Patricia's face. All she could think of was that Luc had been right. She *was* a healer. But of animals, not people.

"Are you all right?" Patricia asked. "You know what happened to you last time…."

"I know. I think I've gotten…stronger. Maybe." Climbing unsteadily to her feet, Sam glanced around the glade and beyond, trying to see into the wavering shadows beneath the trees. "Where's Luc? He didn't…?"

Patricia steadied her. "He left. I watched him go. There's no way he saw anything. You're safe."

Suddenly, Sam was tired of being safe, though she didn't know what else she wanted. The after-effects of the healing were what made her feel so moody and sad, she knew. Temperamental and depleted. She was always like this after she healed even one animal. She had no idea what healing two would do to her this time.

Frankly, she was surprised she hadn't already collapsed. She ought to feel relieved. Luc hadn't seen her. He still didn't know for sure.

Patricia was watching her with concern. "You look really awful, worse than normal. You know you can't heal two so close together. Are you sure this hasn't been too much for you?"

Not wanting to worry her friend, Sam attempted a smile. "So far, so good."

"Okay." Patricia gazed down at Tubby. "How are we going to explain this radically healed dog to Luc and my assistants? All three saw how close to death Tubby was."

"I don't know." Sam rubbed her eyes, her voice cracking. "I'll leave that up to you. Wrap the leg, even though it's healed. Maybe you can keep them from examining him too closely." She took a deep breath, hoping for strength, at least until she got home. "I need to go."

Giving Patricia, who still cradled the small animal, a quick smile, Sam turned and stumbled, nearly dropping her flashlight. Grabbing a slender tree, she righted herself. "Sheesh. Okay, this does seem worse than usual. It's to be expected." She staggered a few more steps before stopping to rest.

"Sam, wait."

But she couldn't. Lifting her hand in a limp wave and shaking with exhaustion, she stumbled toward the road, slipping on leaves and sticks and stones. Sam prayed she could avoid Luc, reach her car, then get in and drive. She had to make it home before passing out. Once there, she planned to tumble into the lavender-scented sheets on her soft bed and fall into oblivion. She felt as if she could sleep for days.

Attempting to start her car, she fumbled with the keys, surprised at how violently her hands were shaking. Her vision grayed and suddenly she couldn't catch her breath. Sucking in shallow gasps of air, she realized driving might not be the best option.

Again, darkness threatened. She got out of her car, legs unsteady. Slipping back into the woods, she used trees to help her stand, her flashlight beam wavering in the darkness.

She had to find Patricia.

Years ago, she'd tried to heal two animals and nearly died. She felt as awful now. Patricia had helped her then.

Patricia would know what to do to help her now.

Chapter 6

Frustrated, Luc paced the parking lot near the small park. All of his kind paced when agitated; doing so was the closest they could come to their other nature without physically changing into a wolf.

Despite every indication otherwise, Sam was not a healer.

The poodle had been as good as dead when they'd found him. If ever Sam would have revealed her healing powers, that would have been the time. Even though they'd made him leave, Luc had seen Patricia getting out her veterinary kit and begin trying to save the animal by conventional means.

Sam had made no effort to help.

If not for the miraculous recovery of the stray cat, Luc would think he'd been wasting his time here.

Several people had come back to the gazebo. They again clustered in small groups, talking and waiting. Mrs. Atkinson was there, too, seated on a bench, still sniffling. Her bright orange-and-pink-flowered dress seemed an odd contrast to the somber mood in the air. Another older woman sat beside her, patting her arm.

Luc waited, too, though in constant motion. Any moment now he expected Patricia to bring the poodle's body out of the woods. He didn't envy whoever had the task of telling Mrs. Atkinson that her Tubby had died.

Again, the urge to change swept through him— again, he pushed it away. He had no time for his wolf, not now. Luc sighed. He didn't envy his own job, either—calling Frank and telling him reports of a healer had been greatly exaggerated.

What about Tomas Barerra? Luc had talked with the young Halfling, heard him tell the same story over and over again. Tomas truly believed that the woman called Sam Warren had touched him and healed him with her hands.

Sam. Luc clenched his teeth. Why he was furious with her, he didn't really know. She'd done nothing, claimed nothing, tried all along to tell him she wasn't what he thought she was, or wanted her to be.

He sighed. Time to pack it in, admit defeat and…

Leave her?

Every instinct rebelled.

Kissing Sam had felt like coming home.

Disgusted with himself and the entire situation, he jammed his hands in his pants pockets and waited.

A moment later, Sam came staggering out of the woods. The others turned to gawk at her, but when she fell, no one moved to assist her.

Except Luc. A few steps carried him to her.

"Let me help you." Slipping one hand under her arm, he steadied her. She gazed up at him with a blank stare, pure exhaustion in her expression and in the hollows under her rich amber eyes.

To his shock, he realized she was weeping. Silent tears made silver streaks down her pale, creamy cheeks. So Tubby had died, as he'd suspected he would. Luc's hand shook as he reached up and wiped away one tear with his finger. "Sam?"

"I've got to go home," she told him thickly, never taking her gaze from his.

"You're in no condition to drive." As she started a weak protest, he lifted her in his arms and carried her to his rental car. Instead of objecting further, she let her head loll against his chest.

By the time he opened the passenger door and placed her in the seat, Sam had fallen asleep.

The drive seemed too short. Pulling up in front of her garage, he let the car idle, and savored her closeness.

Then, reluctantly, he shook her. "Come on, Sam. You're home. Time to wake up."

She didn't stir. He couldn't release her; she lolled against the back of the seat as though boneless.

"Sam?" He felt the first stirring of alarm. "Sam, come on, honey. Wake up."

When nothing happened, full-fledged panic set in. What had happened to Sam in the woods? Digging for his notebook, he found Patricia's cell phone number and punched it in.

In a few short words he told her what had happened.

"Damn, I knew this would…"

"Would what?"

"Take her to the hospital, now."

"Would what, Patricia?"

There was silence for long moments, then she whispered, "Luc?" Her voice shook. "The last time she tried this, years ago, she nearly died. Please. Take her to the emergency room. If you care about her at all, get her some help."

Patricia didn't know it, but he was already on the way.

Screeching into the hospital driveway minutes later, Luc pulled up right in front of the emergency room doors. Ignoring the burly security guard trying to tell him he must move the vehicle, he slammed the car into Park and went around to the passenger side to yank open Sam's door.

Scooping her up in his arms—he'd never realized before how fine-boned she was—he left the rental car running and strode into the hospital.

Someone brought a wheelchair. Luc started to brush past, but realized he'd need his hands free to fill out paperwork. The instant he released his hold on her and settled her in the chair, she was whisked away.

Attempting to follow was futile—three people stepped into his path. A tall woman in dull purple scrubs took his arm and steered him toward a desk. "I'll need you to fill out some paperwork, sir."

Sam's heart stopped twice in as many hours. Each time, they were able to bring her back. Each time, Luc was kept from the room.

His tenuous grip on his temper slipped, fear for Sam making him want to fight his way to her. Something of this must have shown in his expression, frightening the young orderly who'd been given the job of keeping them updated.

Somehow, Luc got himself under control. Still frantic, he paced the halls, his own heart hurting. Did they not understand he *needed* to be with her? She was his *mate*, damn it. He could help her. Somehow. If they'd just let him close.

But when they'd found out he wasn't a relative, they'd barred him from her room. "Intensive care," they told him, and when Patricia arrived they recited the same words to her.

"She doesn't have any family," Patricia told the head nurse and anyone else who would listen. "We're the closest thing she has."

But they wouldn't listen.

His frustration building—he could help her, he *knew* he could help her, somehow, someway—Luc paced and paced.

"We won't be getting any progress reports now,

since you scared the orderly," Patricia said glumly. "You'd better hope Sam doesn't die."

Die? Numb, he stared at her. "They've got her heart beating again," he croaked. "Surely, she won't…"

He couldn't even say the word. His agitation grew, until finally, unable to take any more, he charged the orderly blocking the door to her room, knowing he had to get to her. No matter who or what he had to go through to do so.

With the element of surprise on his side, Luc succeeded in pushing the large man out of the way. Several nurses, doctors, *people* surrounded her bed, working frantically to help her.

More than he needed to breathe, Luc needed to see her. To touch her. To feel the beat of her heart.

But still they sought to keep him from her.

No longer. With no help for it, he shoved his way between two women, taking them by surprise. Something—maybe the look on his face—made them scatter.

With tubes, monitors and wires surrounding her, Sam looked tiny and defenseless, dwarfed in the hospital bed. Her gray skin and still body made Luc pull back his lips in a snarl.

"Mine," he growled, daring them to contradict him. "Mine." His mate.

One man, a doctor, moved to intercept him. "You need to leave so we can help her."

"*I* can help her," Luc told him, though he wasn't sure how.

"Someone call security!"

Before the doctor had finished speaking, one of the machines began to shriek a warning.

"She's arresting again." Focused on saving Sam's life, the medics pushed Luc to the side and again surrounded her.

He had watched enough television to understand what the flat line on the monitor meant. "No," he moaned, starting toward her again.

This time, no one blocked him.

"She's gone," a gray-haired nurse said, eyes soft with pity. "I'm terribly sorry."

He refused to listen, to believe. Not Sam, born to be a healer. Born to be his mate.

One by one the humans filed out of the room. Dimly he registered the room emptying, conscious of Patricia hanging in the doorway. None of that mattered. Only Sam.

Luc let his gaze travel over her. She appeared to be sleeping. They'd turned off all the machines.

She lay still and peaceful, showing no sign of any illness or heart defect or whatever had killed her.

"What was wrong with her?" he rasped, rounding on Patricia so violently she recoiled.

Shaking her head, she began to sob, her shoulders heaving.

Disregarding her for now—he'd have his answers eventually—Luc moved closer to the woman born to be with him. *Sam.*

Her lips were blue, her eyes closed. She was resting peacefully, but not for one night. For eternity.

A howl built in him, and he bit the side of his mouth to keep even a shred of sound from escaping.

His mate.

Now lost to him forever.

What kind of fate had been given to him, to forever lose the ones he loved?

Sam.

Healer, heal yourself.

Please.

Luc bent down to kiss her.

And felt the faintest bit of breath against his lips.

In disbelief, he stared. His heart stuttered, then began to pound.

Behind him, Patricia dropped into a chair, still weeping.

Out in the hall, he could hear nurses talking, asking the doctor if he wanted to sign off yet.

Luc did not summon them back, knowing they would only get in his way.

Bending over her, he gathered her lifeless body in his arms. Slowly, rose and cream began to color her skin, chasing away the gray. Her breath hitched, she coughed and her chest rose and fell.

"What the—?" Jumping up from her chair, Patricia hurried over. With a fierce glare of warning, Luc stopped her from coming too close.

Pressing his lips against Sam's mouth, he gently kissed her. She sighed, stirring, snuggling into his chest.

"What do you think you're doing?" The doctor's voice sounded furious. "Security has been notified and I'm ordering you removed from this hospital."

Luc ignored him. Patricia did not. "She…" Words failed her. She could only point.

Continuing to hold her, Luc kissed the tip of Sam's nose, her jaw and finally the hollow of her throat, where he could see her heartbeat growing stronger.

Two men in uniforms pushed through the doorway. "Arrest that man," the doctor cried. As they moved forward, Luc lifted his head to meet the man's furious gaze.

"What is wrong with you?" the doctor asked. "What did you do to her?"

"She lives," Luc said simply.

"Don't touch him," Sam ordered weakly from the circle of his arms. "He saved my life."

Staring at both of them, Patricia slowly shook her head. "You know, I think he really did."

"The machines all read normal," a nurse said.

The doctor looked from one to the other. Finally, he crossed to Sam, shining a light into her eyes. "I don't know what happened here, but I need to examine you."

Immediately, the nurse chased Luc and Patricia from the room. Luc allowed this, now that Sam was in no danger.

Later, when they'd finished exclaiming over miracles, and had examined every single inch of Sam, they finally allowed Luc back in to see her.

Still resting, she opened her eyes when he entered the room. "I felt you," she told him, her gaze searching his.

"I…" To his mortification, he felt tears fill his eyes. "I didn't want you to die."

"Did you heal me?"

The simple question floored him. "No. I think you healed yourself."

"Ahhh." She closed her eyes, apparently satisfied by his explanation. "I didn't want to leave you."

And she drifted off to sleep.

The next morning, a nurse informed Sam that certain abnormalities in her blood had them wanting to run endless tests on her. Sam allowed it, until Luc told her to make them stop. When Patricia, who seemed to have come to an uneasy truce as far as Luc was concerned, agreed with him, Sam refused all further tests.

"Especially since you already know what's wrong with you," her friend said.

Sam stared. Had Patricia told Luc? With a sinking feeling, she realized she didn't know what had happened while she'd been unconscious.

"Your heart stopped twice," Luc told her, answering her unspoken question as though he'd read her mind. "The third time, they were unable to resuscitate you. By the time I got to you, they'd pronounced you dead."

She couldn't tear her gaze away from his. Despite his expressionless face, she sensed the depth of his vulnerability, hidden below the surface.

Oblivious to the dangerous currents, Patricia stepped forward and took up where Luc had left off. "No one knows what happened. They're calling you a medical miracle. One minute your heart had stopped beating. The next, you drew a breath and appear to be as good as new. Except for whatever you've got in your blood."

"My blood work always comes back abnormal, you know that." Feeling irrationally cross, Sam inhaled. "But no one knows what happened to me?" Staring at Patricia, she knew her friend would understand her question.

"Of course not." Her friend cut her eyes toward Luc. "Though some people are trying awfully hard to find out."

Luc's shuttered expression never changed. His eyes reminded her of the wolves she'd long seen in her dreams.

Feeling as though he could see into her soul, Sam shivered. "I'd like to go home."

"Dr. Leiber won't discharge you. He's hoping to talk you into more blood work."

"He'll sign the paperwork." The certainty in Luc's voice sounded almost like a threat. "Let me go find him." He stalked out of the room.

"What's with him?" Sam asked, feeling his absence as sharply—and absurdly—as though they were tethered at the hip. "Why's he acting so weird?"

Patricia shrugged. "You should have seen him when he thought you'd died." She looked pensive. "I think he really cares about you, Sam. He took you in his arms and held you. That was touching enough, but what killed me were the tears streaming down his face. And when he started kissing you—your mouth, nose, neck, everything—I started crying myself. The whole thing was really intense."

"He *cried?*" Sam couldn't believe Luc had done such a thing. But then, she found it difficult to believe she'd nearly died. All she remembered was falling asleep and then waking up in the hospital with him in a chair by her side.

By her side. With her, where he belonged.

Frowning at the absurd thought, Sam rubbed her eyes. "Tell me you didn't reveal what I did with Tubby."

"Of course not!" From the indignant sound of her voice, Patricia must be shocked she'd even ask such a thing.

"Good," Sam breathed in relief. "Right now I just want to go home and put this entire thing behind me."

"Promise me you'll never try to heal two in one day again."

"What about Tubby? Is he all right?"

"He's better than you. Now come on, promise."

"I'll do my best." Aching and tired, Sam tried to smile, but the effort was too much for her.

The doctor appeared in the doorway, followed by Luc. "What's this nonsense about you wanting to go home?"

Sam nodded. "I'd like that."

"I'm sorry, but I can't release you. Until we find out what caused this problem—"

"I'm leaving."

Frowning, Dr. Leiber looked from Sam to Patricia to Luc. "Isn't anyone going to try and talk some sense into her?"

No one responded. Finally, the doctor sighed. "If your heart arrests again, you will die. The damage will be far too much for you to recover from."

"I'll make sure it doesn't happen again," Sam promised.

If anything, his frown deepened. "This is serious, young lady."

She apologized. Still grumbling, Dr. Leiber signed her release and left. Patricia handed Sam her clothes and helped her to the bathroom. "We'll wait out here."

"I'm driving her home," Luc said. His tone brooked no argument. "She and I need to talk."

Listening through the bathroom door, Sam

waited for her friend to disagree. But this time, Patricia murmured assent. Too drained to summon up her own argument, Sam dressed and emerged from the bathroom.

"Ready?" Luc asked.

When she nodded, he stepped closer. She could swear she felt heat radiating from his powerful body. The urge to touch him, to check for herself, had her wrapping her arms around her middle.

"Take care of yourself." Patricia hugged her. "I'm going to head on home and get some sleep. You do the same now, you hear?"

"I will."

Luc helped Sam to the car, his arm firmly around her waist. Once again, at his touch she felt better. Stronger. Shooting a glance at him to see if he knew, she caught him studying her, a soft look in his eyes.

"I feel better," she said, as he opened the passenger door for her.

"Good." Adjusting her seat belt, he brushed her hair away from her neck, making her shiver. "We do need to talk."

Too tired to dispute it, she leaned her head back against the seat.

Instead of taking her home, he drove to a local steak house.

"Wait here." He disappeared inside. A few moments later he returned, two plastic take-out boxes in hand. "Rare steak," he said as he got back into the car. "There's nothing better for getting your strength up."

Immediately, her mouth began to water. She had to forcibly restrain herself from opening the container and gnawing on the meat as he drove.

What the hell was wrong with her?

Luc took her home, again slipping his arm around her to help her walk to the door. She gave in to the urge to lean her head on his broad shoulder, which made him smile.

Once inside, they sat in the kitchen. Luc watched her while she devoured the steak, so rare the blood made gravy. When she'd finished, he reached across the table and threaded his fingers through hers.

"Sam, I need to ask you again." His low, gentle tone brought irrational tears to her eyes. "Did you heal the cat and Tubby? Was healing them the reason you almost died?"

She bit her lip. Should she tell this man she barely knew? But despite the shortness of their acquaintance, even now, though her heart pounded, she ached for him. No matter what else he might be, he was no stranger. The mysterious connection they shared made her certain of that. The feelings he aroused in her had nothing to do with reason.

Neither did her gift.

If she told him what she could do, would he ever believe she couldn't heal people, especially a sick little girl who was dying?

Then Sam thought of Patricia's niece with chicken pox, and realized all she had to do was invite him to witness the test. If she failed to heal that child, he'd have no choice but to stop looking at her as a potential miracle worker for Lucy.

Of course, considering how this last healing had depleted her, Sam figured the chicken pox could have gone away on its own before she had enough strength to heal again.

Observing Luc through lowered lashes, she saw tenderness and desire rather than impatience in his face. The play of emotions across his features decided her—that and the knowledge that he'd somehow brought her back from the dead, even if he didn't know it.

"Sam? Did you heal those animals?"

Closing her eyes and inhaling, she felt as if she were about to take a flying leap off a ledge without a net. "I did," she whispered. "And Tomas. I healed Tomas Barerra as well."

Luc's sharp intake of breath and sudden stillness told her what her answer meant to him. "Look at me, Sam."

Slowly, she did.

"Ah, Sam." Crossing the distance between them, he kissed her, the driven, desperate kiss of a man drowning. Her fear and hesitation fled as she moved her lips against his. With a glad cry of welcome, she wrapped her arms around his neck and drank as deeply of him as he did of her.

Finally, they broke apart. Resting his forehead against hers, he kissed the tip of her nose. "Is healing always so dangerous for you? You almost died today, all because you healed that poodle."

"Not only the poodle. I healed the cat this morning. Two so close together took too much of my energy." From somewhere she summoned a smile. "I know better than to try to do that again."

He inhaled sharply and she saw the question on his face even before he asked. "Will you come and try to heal Lucy? Without your help, she won't live to see four."

The knife lodged in her stomach twisted. "Luc, I can't heal people. I tried to tell you that. I can only heal animals."

Again he stood. She chanced a glance at him through her lashes. He seemed pensive rather than disturbed or angry.

"You truly don't know."

"Know what?"

As he opened his mouth to reply, his cell phone rang. Frank again. Clenching his jaw, Luc answered.

"I've set you up a meeting," the mayor stated, after the requisite niceties.

"A meeting with whom?"

"A local Pack member out there. They called the New York council and wanted us to arrange something. Not only did they know you were in Texas, but they knew about the potential healer."

Luc rubbed the back of his neck. "Getting their dibs in early, aren't they?"

Frank snorted. "You know politics. You play nice, they'll play nice, and everyone wins."

Luc had never gotten good grades in playing well with others. "I'll do what I can." He jotted down directions Frank gave him to the meeting place and time. Then checking his watch, Luc growled. "You haven't given me much leeway."

"What? You've got a couple of hours. Surely you can get from one end of that town to the other by then."

Though that wasn't the point, Luc let it go. "I'm bringing Sam."

"Who?"

"Samantha Warren. The healer." He snapped the phone closed before Frank could reply, concluding the call.

Watching him, Sam slowly shook her head. "Please don't call me that. You don't know for certain if I am what you're looking for. Actually, I'm not sure I believe any of this myself."

He smiled tightly. "Do you feel well enough to go out to eat?"

"Now? We just had steak."

"In a couple of hours. There's someone I have to meet."

"I think so," she said, then yawned. "Let me take a short nap."

He started to agree, but before he could say anything, Sam had already fallen asleep.

Ninety minutes later, loath to wake her, Luc left her asleep in her bed and got in his car alone. The drive to Jack's Grill on the Water took all of ten minutes. He'd noticed the place before—apparently the owners had done major renovations. In addition to brand-new wood framing and sparkling windows, the streamers and spotlight and huge neon sign proclaiming We're Open Again!! was a huge tip-off.

Since he was early, Luc took a table against the wall with a good view of the door. The dinner crowd hadn't yet filled the place, though there were several guests already seated, enjoying early meals.

When an attractive young couple entered, Luc met the woman's direct gaze and knew. These were the people whom Frank wanted him to meet.

While they crossed the room toward him, he studied them. The woman was tall, blond, beautiful and Pack. The human man at her side couldn't take his eyes off her. Luc knew the feeling—he felt the same way around Sam.

Approaching his table, the woman met his gaze. Her nostrils flared as she checked his scent. A second later, she dipped her chin in a short nod of acknowledgment. "Luc Herrick?"

Standing, he held out his hand. "Pleased to meet you."

"I'm Jewel Reynolds. This is my husband, Colton."

The two men shook hands while she watched with an indulgent smile.

Suddenly, Luc realized where he'd seen her. "You were—"

"Yes." She cut him off, her smile slipping a notch. "Married to a gangster, in the Witness Protection Program and on the run." She took a deep breath. "Now I live here in Anniversary with my mate. We just got back from our honeymoon."

Shaking the other man's hand, Luc grimaced. "I'm sorry. I meant no harm."

"No problem." Colton reached over and massaged his wife's neck. The tension in her slender shoulders seemed to instantly dissolve.

Staring at the two of them, who were leaning into each other as though they'd both found their rock, Luc thought about Jewel's comment that she and Colton were mates. Most shifters dreamed of finding the one, though some pretended to disbelieve any such romantic nonsense.

Luc had always been squarely in the middle, not sure if he believed or not.

Until he'd met Sam. If she was a healer as well as his mate, that would make two myths solid reality.

Mates. He wanted to ask Jewel if she'd known immediately, but wasn't sure if that would offend her.

Taking their seats, they all ordered beers. Once the waitress had moved off, Jewel leaned across the table. "I've kept my membership in the New York Pack, though I'm now also part of Texas. That's why I'm here."

Luc nodded.

"Of course, you understand Texas has a vested interest in this woman who might be a potential healer. The Pack is also very concerned about a stray shifter who's been showing himself to towns-people in this area. I don't have to tell you what a pain in the ass that is. Worse, rumor has it that he's also after the healer."

Chapter 7

That wasn't good news. Frowning, Luc crossed his arms. "How'd he find out about her?"

Jewel shrugged. "I don't know. Probably the same way the Texas Pack did. You know how gossip works. One person tells another, etc. With e-mail, rumors can crisscross the country in hours."

"Have you looked for him?"

"No." She and her husband shared another long glance. "My mate and I just got back. Actually, I was hoping you wouldn't mind taking a look around. Maybe you can sniff him out."

Luc cocked his head, considering. "I can do that," he finally said, glancing at Colton. The human watched the conversation with interest, seemingly unfazed by all this talk of Packs and healers.

"I've adapted," Colton said, not the least bit apologetic.

Jewel reached for her mate's hand. The movement seemed unconscious, as though she craved his touch without deliberate thought.

Luc envied her that.

Something must have shown in his face. Watching him closely, Jewel made a tsking sound. "You aren't married, are you?"

He shook his head, then asked the question he most wanted answered. "How'd you know?" He looked from one to the other. "When you first met, did you both instantly realize the other was meant for you?"

Both Jewel and Colton laughed. "Not hardly," the man drawled. "But something drew me to her. I couldn't seem to stay away."

Intrigued, Luc leaned across the table. "What happened when you learned she could shift? Were you prepared? Or did it just come as one big shock?"

"You're in love with a human?" Disarmingly perceptive, Jewel gave him a sympathetic look.

"Not exactly." No way was he going to explain and let her report back to her Pack that he thought the healer was his mate. Not only would that complicate things, but his claim would supersede any they might make, making the healer's home Pack the one in New York.

Just thinking about this made him scowl. Politics like this he didn't want to get involved in. Ever.

The waitress came and took their orders. All three ordered the largest steaks available, cooked rare. Once she departed, both Colton and Jewel stared at Luc expectantly, waiting for his answer.

Instead, he steered the conversation back to the reason they'd met. The healer.

"Do either of you know her?"

Jewel shook her head. "I'm just getting to know people here. I had a rocky start."

"That's the understatement of the year." Colton chuckled. "I know her, and I can't believe y'all are talking about Sam Warren. I've known her ever since I moved to town. Nice lady. But she's just a regular woman—a librarian, for Pete's sake—not some mystical healer. Maybe you've gotten her mixed up with Patricia Lelane, the vet. Now she's a healer if I ever saw one."

When neither Luc nor Jewel laughed, Colton

raised his hands. "Fine. Assuming you know what you're doing, I'll stay out of it."

The steaks arrived and they all dug in. Luc and Jewel ran a close race, devouring theirs before Colton had eaten half of his.

"You're not wolves, you're pigs," he snorted.

Luc grinned and checked his watch. Tossing three ten-dollar bills on the table, he stood. "I enjoyed meeting you two. Dinner is on me."

"Let me know if you find out anything about this rogue shifter, okay?" Jewel asked, her expression concerned.

"I will."

With a lot to think about, Luc drove back to check on Sam.

She still slept. He sat by her bed in the darkness and watched her, marveling at the connection they shared. Did she feel it, too? He thought of the way she'd kissed him, and knew she must.

Feeling both exhilarated and lonely, Luc went outside. The moon hung weakly in the November sky, barely a sliver. He walked the length of Sam's backyard, heading toward the trees. Once he'd reached the woods, he removed his clothes, stashing them in the deep crotch of a tree.

Cross-legged, he took a seat on the ground. Tasting the cold night air, he smelled deer and rabbit and raccoon, but no other predators.

Yet. A wolf's nose worked infinitely better than a human's.

One last look around and Luc pushed himself to his knees. Crouching low on all fours, he concentrated and began the change. The time had come to hunt.

As his bones lengthened and his body reformed, joy filled him. The wolf had been forced into submission far too long. Now he pushed harder against the human cage than he'd ever done before.

Luc *erupted* into wolf, rather than changed.

Though flashes of light always accompanied a change, this time the color was intense, fluorescent and blinding. Releasing his last shred of humanity, Luc gave himself over to wolf, and the change became complete.

Wolf, Luc rose to his feet and tasted the breeze. He smelled only November—the hint of a cold snap hovering to the north, the acrid taste of smoke left from someone who'd burned leaves earlier.

Glorying in his strength, he roamed the forest for hours, glad to feel the moist earth beneath his paws, constantly searching the air for the scent of another shifter.

But though he revisited all the areas where the werewolf had been seen, he had no luck.

Once, deep within the woods near a fast-moving stream, he found a spot where a campfire had burned, but the faded scent was completely human. It could have belonged to hikers or campers. No, he was looking for the trace of shifter.

He'd talked to several people in town and knew where each claimed to have seen the werewolf. Yet as he traveled to each and every place in his wolf form, not once did he pick up a single hint that told him *shifter*.

Luc wasn't aware of a way any shifter could completely obliterate his or her scent. Perhaps the rumors were wrong.

Finally, as the winter moon hung cold and distant in the inky sky, he changed back to human form, found his clothes and climbed in his rental car to head back to Sam's. He'd learned absolutely nothing.

Time crept slowly forward, like a tortoise looking for a pond. He grew impatient, waiting for the leaves to change. Instead, he woke one morning to find most of them dead, clinging stubbornly to the trees as though they meant to remain that way forever.

Forever. He felt as if he'd waited for the Halfling to reveal herself for an eternity. Waited with his patience unraveling like a frayed rope, slivers and chunks pulling free until an entire lifetime became encompassed in the threads.

Though only days had passed, his life was now measured in days. The time had come. He was dying. Nothing could save him but hope. Nothing could help him but a healer.

He must grab the woman. Now, when the days merged into nights and the weeks into months. Now, when he could no longer tell whether he was man or wolf or both or none. All he knew was that he wearied of the wait.

He grunted, for a moment forgetting what shape he wore. Glancing down at his forelimbs, he saw pale skin and ragged nails. Human, then. Good.

Now he would succeed. And live. Even the scrabbly trees whispered this in the wind. The time had come to make another move.

Dimly aware of Luc returning, Sam struggled to wake enough to greet him. But her body craved sleep as much as she craved his touch, and she couldn't make her eyes open or her voice work.

The next thing she knew, sunlight streamed in the windows. Stretching, she realized Luc lay beside her, one leg over hers.

Instantly, desire flared. He resembled nothing so much as a dark angel, beautiful and sensual. Even as she debated bending in for a kiss, he opened his eyes.

"Morning." His smile made her stomach flip-flop.

"You stayed with me." The minute she spoke, she regretted opening her mouth.

"Except for a brief walk through the woods, yes." His pupils darkened. "Do you always look this good when you wake up in the morning?"

As she tried to come up with a witty reply, he sat up, narrowing his eyes. "What is that?" Lifting his head, his nostrils flared. "Do you smell—?"

"Smoke." She sniffed the air, too, hoping the odor came from someone burning leaves. No such luck. A quick glance down the hallway revealed wisps of smoke drifting from underneath the closed closet door.

She climbed out of bed and headed toward it.

"Wait." Luc grabbed her arm. "You get the cat and go outside. Call 911 from your cell phone. Let me see if I can contain it."

She didn't want to leave her home, but he made sense. Scooping up the agitated cat, she headed for the door. Halfway there, something exploded. A shower of sparks, then black, pungent smoke poured from the doorway adjacent to the den.

"My kitchen!" Sam reversed direction, but Luc's broad-shouldered body intercepted her.

"Outside."

"But—" The smoke grew thicker, making it hard to breathe.

"Go. That sounded like a grenade. Wait for me outside." He disappeared into the thick cloud of smoke.

Coughing, she reached for the door handle. Stumbling outside, eyes watering, she placed the cat on the grass and doubled over, gasping for air. Beside her, the cat bristled and coughed, hacking smoke from his lungs.

Flames billowed up into the sky. The entire back of her house appeared to be on fire.

Another explosion rocked the night. Luc! Had he gotten out?

A maroon van pulled up to the curb. Ignoring it, Sam struggled to straighten, watching for Luc, praying he would appear on the porch any second. The cat darted off, crouching behind a shrub.

"Are you all right?" An older man wearing sunglasses and a cowboy hat over long, silver hair, came up to her. When Sam looked up and opened her mouth to respond, he jabbed something sharp in her arm.

"What the—!"

"Sedative, sweetheart. You're going to sleep. When you wake up, you're going to heal me."

What? Sam tried to move away, but the drug had already begun to take effect. The man's image wavered as she felt her legs go boneless. She slid to the grass while the cat watched from under his bush.

Help me! Luc...

As if she'd summoned him, Luc appeared on the porch, the blaze behind him illuminating his powerful figure. Sam tried to lift her hand toward him, gasping as the stranger grasped her under the arms and began dragging her to the van. She slipped in and out of consciousness, aware only that she mustn't let the stranger get her into his vehicle.

The sound of Luc's feet pounding the earth echoed her heartbeat. She opened her eyes to blurrily register his flying leap as he tackled the other man. The two of them tangling on the lawn were the last things she saw and heard before the drug finally claimed her and the world went black.

* * *

The gray-haired stranger went down far too easily, and too late to soften the blow. Luc realized the man was hiding his frailty behind baggy clothes. At least the bastard let go of Sam, who promptly moaned and sank to the ground beside the still-as-death cat.

"Do you not realize what she is? Let me have the healer," the man said, scrambling to his feet.

In that instant, Luc got a whiff of his scent and growled. Pack. The other man was Pack. A Halfling. Worse, he'd called Sam a healer. That meant he knew what she might be able to do.

Was this man the werewolf who'd been terrorizing Anniversary?

The stranger seemed to realize Luc had discerned his true nature. He backed away and took off for the van. Luc started to follow, but Sam moaned again and he went to her instead.

When he reached her, what he saw on the ground beside her nearly stopped his heart. A syringe.

Hell hounds.

Snarling in fury, he spun and sprinted for the van. With a squeal of tires, it pulled away just as he reached for the door handle.

He cursed again, committing the license plate

to memory. Grabbing his cell phone, he dialed 911 and reported the explosion and the van, but not the abduction attempt. He hung up without identifying himself.

Once he'd finished, he scooped up Sam and deposited her in the backseat of his car. He returned and made a cursory search for the cat. The animal must have run off. He'd call Patricia and have her come out and find it.

Just as Luc would let the authorities deal with the fire. No way was he leaving Sam in anyone else's hands.

At first, he started to take her to his motel room. But then he realized a lot of people, Patricia included, might believe he'd set the fire, and send the authorities after him. Even though he'd done nothing, time spent in a police station lockup was time he could not afford. Especially with Sam unconscious.

No, his motel room was no longer safe, at least not until she woke and could tell the authorities the truth.

Even then, the Halfling who'd tried to grab her might still be a dangerous threat. He'd used a syringe, though if he wanted Sam to heal him, Luc wagered the effects of whatever drug he'd selected would be only temporary.

The question of how the Halfling had known

about Sam remained. As far as Luc knew, only two Packs were aware of her potential—the New York Pack and the Texas Pack, both of which disallowed him. Though word might have spread, it had only been a little over three weeks since Sam had healed Tomas. No way would the news have made it to outsiders so quickly.

The other man had been a Halfling. If not Texas or New York, then what Pack? Though he'd looked vaguely familiar, Luc couldn't place him. He'd had the look of an outsider, an outcast. And, if he turned out to be the legendary werewolf stalking Anniversary, he'd broken several major Pack laws.

Sam made a sound, reminding Luc he had more immediate problems. He drove to the edge of town and parked on the shoulder of the road, trying to decide. He'd left only a few changes of clothes in the motel room, and his toiletries could be replaced.

While he debated, he placed a call to Carson.

"How's Lucy?" he asked. The silence on the other end of the line tied his stomach in knots.

"Not good," Carson finally replied, his voice vibrating with tension. "What's keeping you, man?"

Luc started to explain about the fire and the failed abduction attempt, but some instinct made him ask another question instead. "What are you not telling me?"

His friend gave a weary sigh. "I just got off the phone with Dr. Nettles. Lucy's slipped into a coma. They aren't optimistic about her chances."

Closing his eyes, Luc swallowed. "Give it to me straight."

Tears came through in the other man's voice. "They say she doesn't have long—" His voice broke. Clearing his throat, he finished. "She doesn't have long to live."

"What? A month? A week? How much longer?" Luc couldn't take an unconscious—and uncooperative—woman on a plane. Plus, he needed at least a day or two to make Sam aware of her heritage. "Give it to me straight."

Carson spoke in the unemotional tone of a man who no longer believed in miracles. "They've given her a week to ten days, Luc. No more. How quickly can you get the healer here?"

"Give me two days," Luc said.

Carson started to comment, then drew a breath. "Please get her here as quickly as you can. She's our last hope."

Luc took I-45 north, heading out of town toward Dallas. He'd pick up I-30 there and head northeast, hoping to make the Arkansas border before dark. Surely once he explained the situation, Sam would understand.

Curled up in the backseat, Sam slept. Luc drove until his eyesight blurred, drove until the winter moon hung like a chilly sliver in the inky sky. As each hour passed and Sam didn't stir, his worry grew. Whatever drug the Halfling had injected into her was strong.

When he reached Texarkana, he found a cheap motel and stopped for the night. He'd have a full day tomorrow when Sam woke and demanded an explanation. She wouldn't take kindly to him carrying her off without her knowledge.

The fire, the stranger trying to grab her, these events conspired to give him reasons to get her out of town. But, though she'd been with him when the fire had started, once he started talking about Pack and shape-shifters, he wouldn't blame her if she suspected *he'd* set the fire.

At the motel office, he left her in the car while he checked in. Then, driving around to the back and their room, he left the car running while he unlocked the door and propped it open.

She woke when he turned the ignition off,

barely. As he lifted her out of the car, she mumbled something about the cat and snuggled into him. His chest tightened.

Mate. One more secret he had to share with her.

Carrying her into the motel room, he rehearsed what he'd say once she regained consciousness. Bad enough to wake in a strange bed with him beside her, but once she learned they were in Arkansas on their way to New York...

Lucy. He must think of Lucy. With her life at stake, saving her came first, not the wishes of the woman he now knew to be the only one for him.

Once he'd settled Sam in bed, he covered her with the light blanket and told himself he wouldn't touch her again. Instead of watching her sleep, he took a seat in the hard-backed chair at the desk and stared at the phone. Should he call Frank and tell him what he'd done?

How long he sat motionless with Sam's soft breathing the only sound in the room, he didn't know. Her scent, light and floral and earthy, seemed to fill the space, just from her presence. He felt oddly content, strangely at peace.

A noise from outside, low and guttural like a banshee's moan, roused him. Curious, he went to the window, peering around the curtain. Outside, the wind had picked up, sending the bare tree branches flying like frenetic, grasping claws. The moon had disappeared, replaced by huge, roiling clouds.

A November storm. Arkansas got snow, he knew, but he also remembered reading reports of ice storms snarling electrical lines, downing trees and destroying homes.

Fat raindrops spattered the window. They came down hard and angrily, as if a warning of a gale yet to come. Lightning flashed; a few seconds later came the sharp crack of thunder. So far, only rain. Luc let the curtain fall. How ironic! The stormy weather mirrored the tumult inside him.

Sam slept through it all.

She dreamed of wolves. Packs of them, streaming across a flat, grassy plain under the silver light of a half-moon. In her dream, longing filled her, and she realized she only watched from a distance, rather than running with them as she wanted. Though she tried and tried, she stood rooted in place, aching to join them, wild and fierce and free. Alone, she could only watch. And hurt.

She woke with a start, perspiration dampening her T-shirt. She'd had this same dream before, many times, one of the many variations in her apparently endless repertoire of wolf dreams.

And now, she saw Luc Herrick in them. Intense, mysterious Luc, with his bedroom eyes and easy smile. She hadn't felt so drawn to a man since…

Refusing to even think her ex-husband's name, she blinked in the bright light and tried to focus. The smell seemed off. Wrong. Gradually, the ugly green-and-orange bedspread registered. This was not her bed. Nor her room.

Over there—Luc dozed in an ugly purple armchair.

With wolves still in her thoughts, Sam's first instinctive reaction was a low growl. This woke Luc.

"How are you feeling?" His voice sounded gentle.

Narrowing her eyes, Sam swung her legs over the side of the bed. "Confused. My mouth tastes like cotton and I'm obviously hallucinating. Why else would I wake in a strange, tacky room with this cat and you?"

"We're in a motel room off I-30."

"What?" Frowning, she remembered. "The fire. And that awful man with the needle." Glancing down at her arm, she saw the red mark where he'd jabbed her. "Luc, what the heck is going on?"

He smiled then, the sad smile of a man who

didn't have much to lose anymore. "I've got a lot of explaining to do."

"I'll say." She stood and waited until the room stopped moving before crossing to the window and separating the curtains. "Is that…snow?"

"Sometime during the night, the rain turned into snow."

"In November? In Texas? No way."

"We're not in Texas."

Sliding her gaze around the room, she tried to slow her racing heart. "How much is left of my house?"

Luc shook his head. "Nothing."

"That's why we're in a hotel room?"

"Partly, yes. Sam, do you remember what that man said to you before you passed out?"

She frowned. "Something about going to sleep and then…" Closing her eyes, she groaned. "Healing him."

When Luc didn't respond, she opened her eyes to look at him. "Did he cause the fire?"

"Probably. Apparently he's ill and believes you have the power to make him well."

"Like you do with your friend's daughter."

When he looked at her, heat and sorrow blazed from his eyes. "I spoke to Carson last night.

Lucy's slipped into a coma. They've given her a week to live."

"So you thought you'd kidnap me while I was unconscious?" Anger and a feeling of pity were strong enough to make her cross the room to Luc and face him. "Why?"

He said simply, "So Lucy can live."

"She still might make it. People awaken from comas all the time."

"Not with her kind of brain tumor. I'll ask you again. Will you come to New York and heal her?"

Unable to look away, she swallowed. "My gift doesn't work on people. Only animals."

His wry grimace told her he, too, recalled this was exactly where they'd been when the fire had started.

She remembered something else. "You said that I truly didn't know. Don't know what?"

"Your heritage. Remember what I told you before, about the shape-shifters?"

She nodded. How could she forget? "The things you can't disprove."

He looked pleased. "Exactly. To put it as simply as possible, there are those who are half-human and half-animal. Conventional medicine can't heal them. Lucy is one of them. She's a Halfling, and can change shape."

Stomach churning, Sam didn't know what to say. Luc had entered the realm of the supernatural. Supernaturally insane, that is. If not for her dreams, she'd want to run away from him as fast as she could.

"This is where you come in. In our lore, we have read of those who are born with a rare gift— the ability to heal these Halflings with their touch."

"Only Halflings? Not full-blooded, er, shape-shifters?"

"No, we can heal ourselves. But you are needed to heal the others."

"Like I do with animals."

"Exactly. They—you—are called healers."

Digesting this in silence, Sam remembered Patricia's warning about keeping an open mind. She sighed. "Okay. Let's suppose I take your story at face value. If there are such things as shape-shifters, and healers to heal them, how would you identify one? In other words, why me?"

He gave her a look full of so much tenderness, her breath caught.

Doggedly, she continued. "You mentioned heritage. Does that have something to do with all this?"

Luc nodded. "Yes. Now comes the difficult part."

Chapter 8

That got her attention even more, if possible. "More difficult than what you've already told me?"

"Yes." He ran his hand through his hair. "How much do you know about your family?"

She frowned. "Not a lot. My mother worked two jobs to raise me. She never spoke of any family, either on her side or my father's."

"What did she tell you about your father?"

"He left when I was two. My mother rarely spoke of him."

"Did you ask?"

"Once or twice. All she'd say was that he wasn't a good man. Why?"

"Your father was…" Luc took a deep breath. "A full-blooded shifter. He could become a wolf. When he left you and your mother all those years ago, he returned back east to his Pack."

"Pack?" The word felt both foreign and wonderful on her tongue. "As in *wolf* pack?"

Luc nodded.

She thought of her dreams. "My father's a werewolf."

"Yes."

"My mother hated him."

Luc said nothing.

"Do you think she knew?" She watched him closely.

"Possibly. Most likely."

"Assuming I believe you, which I don't, why wouldn't my mother tell me?"

He shook his head. "There could be a lot of reasons, Samantha. Especially if she hated that about him. Obviously, your mother wanted you to be human."

"I *am* human." She bristled. "Though I've dreamed about wolves for years, I know for a fact that I've never changed into one. Even," she amended, unable to keep a trace of sadness from her voice, "in my dreams."

"I'm sorry." Placing a hand on her shoulder, he drew her closer. "But whatever gene that enables us to change, gives you the power to heal."

As always, his touch soothed. She took a deep breath. "What about my father? Do you know him? Even though he abandoned his family and made no attempt to contact me, as a child I always wanted to meet him."

"I know *of* him. My pack researched your heritage. He was killed in a fire five years ago. There was an investigation—they thought he might have been murdered—but no killer was ever found."

Just like that, her foolish hopes for family instantly evaporated. Sorrow for a man she'd never known wasn't easy to come by. Still, she'd spent much of her life wishing for a father who'd never wanted her to return to her life. Now, she mourned the loss of that irrational expectation.

Nervously, she moistened her dry lips. "Do you know if I have any living family?"

"I'm sure you must. The Pack is quite large."

Family. In this…Pack. She thought of her dream wolves and how she could never run with them.

If she was half shifter, that meant she ought to

be able to change into a wolf, too. And finally, finally run with the others.

If only life were so simple.

"I'm a…?"

"A Halfling."

Her gaze flew to his. He watched her with silent expectation. Only years of dreaming of wolves kept her from running away.

What did he expect? Did he really think she was going to shrug and say, "Okay, cool?" Logical thinking had always served her well in the past, with her books and her library. "But that doesn't make any sense. You said Halflings can change into wolves. So wouldn't I be able to become a wolf, too?"

"Most Halflings can change. Healers are different."

Was that a hint of wonder in his deep, velvety voice? Despite his confident expression, she sensed his vulnerability. His need and fears and desires. Her feelings for him, this mysterious man she'd known only a few days, intensified by the hour.

Even now, while he tried to convince her to believe in his insanity, she wanted him. Wanted him with a fierce hunger she'd never felt before. Wanted him so badly she licked her lips and drew her breath in with a hiss of raw need.

Attuned to her as he was, his eyes darkened, reflecting her own craving.

That look sent a tremor through her.

"Sam." Whispering her name, he took a step toward her before collecting himself. When he shook his head, sending his dark hair flying, the movement reminded her of the wolf he claimed to be able to become.

"Now is not the time," he murmured.

Because he was right, she nodded and struggled to find her voice. "Tell me more about this Pack."

"Packs are our way of governing ourselves. Each state has one, and there are regional Packs, and a national one as well. We even elect a president every four years, the same way you do in Washington."

"There are that many of you?"

"Yes."

Incredulous, she rubbed her neck. "Where? How is such a thing possible without anyone knowing?"

"Oh, a few humans have discovered the truth. Most have been labeled crackpots. They write books and give lectures, but no serious-thinking person takes one word seriously."

"And you, with your books to discredit them, is that a form of cover, too?"

"Of course." He smiled, the sheer masculine beauty of him making her insides clench. "Why else would I do such a thing?"

Not entirely convinced, she hugged her arms close to her body. "Luc, I'm sorry to ask this, but are you in some sort of cult or something? Is that what this is all about?"

She could have sworn she saw a flash of hurt in his dark eyes. "Why would you say such a thing?"

She refused to look away. "Because nothing you've said makes any sense."

A muscle worked in his jaw. She longed to reach up and place her hand along his cheek.

Some of her thoughts must have again communicated to him. He sighed once more. "I'm sorry to disappoint you. No cult. In time, you might find it easier to accept an alternate version of reality, if you keep an open mind. We shifters are a race. Just as regular humans are." He paused, swallowing hard. "And finding a healer is very significant to us."

There was something in his voice…an awful ache, remembered sorrow. She felt the effect of his grief as if it were her own. More than worry and fear over a small child's fate, there was something dark and hurtful in his recent past.

Somewhere, somehow, Luc had suffered greatly.

She knew an instant of regret that she hadn't been there then to help him through it.

"What about you?" she asked quietly. "Other than Lucy, what is your personal stake in all of this? Why did your Pack send you, specifically, to find a healer?"

"I wanted to come. Two years ago, I lost my half brother to cancer. Standing by, unable to help or ease his pain, reduced to merely watching while he suffered, was the most awful thing I've ever experienced." Luc took a deep, shuddering breath. "They asked me because they felt I needed hope. They were right."

"Hope?"

"I didn't believe in much of anything anymore," he said, his voice harsh. "Until I met you. You're my—" Breaking off, he ran a hand through his hair, his eyes dark and unreadable. "And because my best friend's daughter is dying. If there's even the slightest chance you are a true healer, I cannot stand by and allow Lucy to die."

Though Sam knew he'd left something unsaid, something important, she wasn't sure she wanted to hear it. He'd given her enough to think about, enough strangeness and worry and fear. But Lucy was who really mattered now. Whatever Sam thought about Luc's stories, that little girl was in real trouble. "Of course I'll go," she said.

Looking relieved, he glanced at his watch. "There's an airport in Little Rock. It'd be much quicker to fly."

"I can't…" She swallowed, feeling slightly foolish, but not caring. "I never fly. Not anymore, not since the plane crash." Even thinking of setting foot on a plane made her break out in a cold sweat, despite the day's chill. She took a deep breath. "How long will the trip take if we go by car? A day?"

"From here to New York? More like two, and that's driving nonstop, with no traffic problems."

"With us taking turns at the wheel, we can drive straight through." Because he still appeared uncertain, she added, "That's the only way I'll agree to go."

Narrowing his eyes, he considered her. "All right," he said.

Immediately, some of her terror eased. She rolled her shoulders, massaging her neck. "Great. Thanks. I wish I knew more about Halflings and healers, those legends you mentioned."

"In that backpack on the backseat are several reference books on healers. If you'd like, once we have daylight, you're welcome to read them."

"I'd enjoy that. Now I need to call Patricia. She'll be worried sick."

Wordlessly, he handed her his cell phone.

Sam dialed the number to the vet clinic from memory. One of the assistants put her right through to her friend.

"Where are you? I found your cat after the fire. He's sick, but are you all right? Has he hurt you?"

"I'm fine." Sam kept her voice soothing. "Has who hurt me?"

"Luc Herrick. He burned your house down, you know."

"No, he didn't. There's a lot you don't know. But Luc was there with me when an explosion started a fire."

"Sam, come on. People are even starting to think *he* might be the werewolf."

Instantly, though Sam didn't know how he could have heard, Luc shook his head. "Tell her about the man who tried to grab you."

"I will." She made a motion meant to indicate that she'd like some privacy.

Inclining his head, Luc disappeared into the bathroom. A moment later, the shower started.

She tried not to think of him naked, with water sluicing off his trim, muscular body. "I'm with him."

"Luc? Why?"

Sam filled in the details of Lucy's illness and what Luc thought she could do. "I'm going to New York with him."

"You're doing *what?*" Patricia shrieked. "Have you lost your mind? You've only known this man a week. He gives you some bullshit story about a sick kid, and you're going off with him?"

Put that way, it did sound rather stupid. However, Patricia didn't know they'd already started the trip, or that Luc believed Sam was a healer. Nor about the strange and dangerous man who'd tried to snatch her. Yet.

"He told you *what?*"

Sam repeated Luc's story about her father and the Pack.

"He's crazy!" Patricia exclaimed. "I never would have believed it, but the to-die-for Luc Herrick is certifiably nuts."

Sam felt obligated to defend him. Why, she had no idea. "There might be some truth to what he says."

"Something in your voice…" Patricia said suspiciously. "What else is going on between you two?"

"He kissed me again," Sam blurted, blushing when she realized she wanted him to do more. Much more.

"How? A peck on the cheek kind of kiss, or a teeth-touching, tongue-in-throat, where-have-you-been-all-my-life kind of kiss, like he did when I was over?'

Sam could feel her face heating ever worse. "The second."

"Oh. Ohhh. Now I understand why you're not laughing about this. Part of you wants to believe it."

"Maybe. Actually, part of me wants to believe *some* of it. Not the bit about my father being a werewolf."

"Hmm." Patricia's tone was thoughtful. "Maybe there *is* some truth to what he says. After all, you *can* heal animals."

Sam closed her eyes. "I know," she said. "That's what makes all this even more frightening." She told her friend about the man who'd tried to grab her. "I think he set the fire. Luc saved my life."

"You're serious about going with him?"

"I am. I have to. Especially now."

"I would think after all this, you'd have strong second thoughts. Doesn't the weirdness aspect bother you at all?"

It did. Sam didn't know which bothered her more—Luc's crazy claim of being a shape-shifter, or the deep, soul-searing kisses they'd shared. She suspected her worry came from equal measures of both.

But where she could dismiss the first as the product of a fertile imagination, she couldn't stop thinking about the second.

Why had he kissed her?

Worse, why had she kissed him back? And why did her body ache for his?

"I have to go with him," she repeated.

This time, her friend was silent. Finally, she spoke. "Please, Sam. Reconsider."

"I can't. You should have seen Lucy's picture. She's so adorable and she's only three and she's dying. She's at Sloan-Kettering in New York." Sam pleaded with her friend to understand. "There's no way I can turn my back on a terminally ill child."

"But you're going on a cross-country road trip with a man you don't even know. Come on, Sam. You have more sense."

What could she say to make her friend understand? "You're forgetting he knew about Tomas."

"You're trusting him because of that? You mean you think he…that is, the wolf pup actually was…"

"A werewolf?" Interesting how Sam could say this with so much aplomb, when ten minutes ago she'd been thinking Luc was stark, raving crazy. "That would also explain how Tomas got out of the locked clinic."

"But Sam, this…"

"Sounds nuts."

"Well, yeah. But…"

Sam knew what she was thinking. "I can heal animals. You told me to keep an open mind." She took a deep breath, reluctant to sound too enthusiastic. Patricia knew her well enough to detect falsehood. On the other hand, if she let her friend know how worried she was, Patricia would insist she come home.

"He also said he knew about my father. He said he'd tell me my family history."

"Like dangling a carrot in front of a starving rabbit."

"No fair. You know how much I long for family."

"But Sam, have you thought about what you might do to that little girl's parents if you show up there, claiming you can heal their sick child, when you don't know if you can? We never did the test."

"I've thought of that. But if he's right, this little girl is part animal."

"The shape-shifter stuff again."

"Right. He actually thinks I'm one of them. Part human and part animal."

"Honey, we're all part animal. That doesn't mean I buy into his story."

"I know." Sam sighed. "I don't know if I can really help, but I have to try. I'm worried about my job, though. I've got to make sure the library is covered while I'm gone."

"I'll call John at city hall first thing in the morning. Don't worry about that."

"Thank you."

"I still think you're making a mistake. So help me, if that Luc is lying to you…"

"Don't worry. I can't see what he'd gain."

"Girl, he's taking you up north. Anything can happen up there." Patricia's voice brightened as she thought of something. "Have you checked him out on the Internet?"

"No."

"Hold on. Let me do a search." She placed the phone down and Sam heard her mouse clicking.

Curious, Sam waited.

"Wow." Returning to the phone and letting out a low whistle, Patricia sounded impressed. "I knew he was an author, but not that he'd written so many nonfiction books. All debunking paranormal myths like the Loch Ness Monster, vampires, zombies, ghosts and…"

"Werewolves," Sam said. "He's working on a book debunking werewolves." She waited for her friend to make the connection.

In a second, she did.

"Wow. That makes perfect sense, if there really are werewolves and they don't want people to know. Luc might be their official spin doctor."

"True."

Patricia went silent for a second or two, then her voice rose with excitement. "I know. Maybe you should ask for proof."

Sam bit her lip. "Proof how?"

"If he's a werewolf, make him show you. If he can't, then you'll know he's a liar."

"And if he can?"

"Then you've got more trouble than I know how to handle. Have you considered purchasing a weapon, a small pistol like a derringer or something? For protection, just in case?"

"I think there's a waiting period and even if I could buy a gun, I wouldn't even know how to use it."

"It's not that difficult. Point and squeeze the trigger."

"No." Sam waved dismissively, then remembered Patricia couldn't see her. "I can't imagine shooting an insect, never mind a person."

"You could if your life was in danger, believe me."

"Maybe, but a gun would be pointless. A pistol wouldn't do me any good, anyway."

"What do you mean?"

"I'd need silver bullets, remember? Ordinary bullets don't work on werewolves."

Despite the ever increasing snowfall, after his shower, Luc kept stepping outside into the white cold. The first few times he did, he returned a moment later looking both sheepish and fiercely desperate. When he wasn't dashing out into the snow like a kid trying to spy on Santa Claus, he paced in front of the small hotel room's window.

His restless agitation had become a palpable thing.

Finally, Sam couldn't stand it any longer. "What on earth is wrong with you? You're reminding me of a bloodhound that thinks he smells something interesting outside and wants to chase it."

At her description, Luc froze, then slowly nodded. "You've pegged how I feel exactly right."

He sighed, searching her face. "Sam, I don't want to frighten you, but it's been awhile since I've changed into a wolf. I don't know how much longer I can contain the urge. I think it might be better if I stay outside for a while."

Proof. Patricia had told her she should ask for proof.

"What if I want to see you shape-shift?"

He gave her a look so intense, so full of emotional baggage, that Sam wanted to go to him and kiss it away.

He glanced once more at the window, at the swirling white storm outside. "Are you sure?"

"Yes." She swallowed hard. Then, more firmly, she repeated, "Yes. I want to see."

He held himself immobile, hands clenched into fists for a moment. Then he reached for her, pulling her close and placing her hand on his heart.

"Feel."

His heart beat strongly and frantically, far too fast for anyone who hadn't been running.

Was this the beginning of his…change?

Heat coiled low in her belly and her breath caught. Her desire must have shown in her eyes, because she saw a reflection of her need in his face.

"Luc…"

"Kiss me," he growled. "Kiss me now, before I run out into the snow."

She needed no second urging. The instant their lips touched, she felt seared, as though she'd stepped from snow into an inferno.

Why was it always this way between them?

The kiss started deep, shattering her self-control. She knew then that she wanted to make love to this man—fast and furious, slow and sensual, both ways, all ways....

Luc made a sound low in his throat. Sam paused. The rumbling growl didn't seem completely human.

Shocked, she opened her eyes and blinked...and wondered why thousands of glittering fireflies were swirling in a frenetic dance before her face. No. Not possible. This was November and she was inside a motel room in the middle of nowhere. There weren't any fireflies at this time of year.

Yet the zigzagging colors tickled her eyelids.

She tore her mouth from his and backed away.

Surrounded by so many flickering lights that she could barely see him, Luc made another sound, an animal cry. Panting, he ran to the door, yanked it open and tore out of the room. The sparkling light show went with him.

Curious, despite her fear and the cold, Sam grabbed the jacket he'd left behind and followed. Ahead she could see the swirling lights dancing in the whiteness, a flash of color through the blowing snow.

Wrapping Luc's jacket around herself tightly, she trudged after him. The snow was deep enough that she could follow his tracks, though new accumulation soon began to fill them in. Luc and his light show had disappeared into the woods, where the darkness seemed more complete. Still, she kept going, stopping only when she reached a large trampled area in a glade.

There, she found Luc's clothes piled on a rock. His socks and shoes, slacks and shirt, even his expensive loafers were there, becoming dusted with white.

She remembered what he'd said earlier about being naked save for wolf fur.

Part of her wanted to see his other self, his alter ego. At the same time she wanted to run back to the motel.

Turning in a slow circle, Sam realized the footsteps seemed to stop. Or…change. Instead of human prints, she saw animal prints in the snow. Wolf prints.

No way! Yet there they were.

For Sam, reality seemed to shift, then tilt on its axis.

Werewolves—shape-shifters—were real. And she was half shifter.

Something inside her thrilled at the thought. Would Luc know her, recognize her, when he was a wolf? Would she be in any danger?

A snuffling noise made her turn. Fifty feet away, a majestic, pewter-colored wolf waited. The same wolf she'd seen a hundred times in her dreams.

"Luc?" She could have sworn the animal tilted his head. No. Freaking. Way.

He'd told her. She'd listened. She'd even told herself this was fascinating and thrilling. In the abstract.

But evidently, she hadn't really believed. Until now.

Luc had become a wolf.

Chapter 9

How was this possible? Staring at the magnificent animal in front of her, Sam wondered at her absence of fear. A wolf was a wild animal, a predator, and she could be in danger.

But not from him. Never from him.

This was Luc.

He had told only the truth. She was involved in this now, like it or not. This was her heritage.

Again, as in her dreams, she knew a fierce longing to become a wolf, to change, to run wild and free. According to Luc, such a thing wasn't in the cards for her. She'd never changed, nor would she. She'd been born for an entirely different purpose. To heal.

Starting with a sick little girl.

And ending, perhaps, with Luc. She could bridge the abyss inside him. *Ah, Luc.* With a flash of blinding clarity, she realized that for her, everything would always come down to Luc.

Again she looked at the wolf. Luc's chocolate eyes gazed back at her from the regal lupine face.

Uncertain, afraid, exhilarated all at once, she took a step closer. Then another. Soon, she was near enough to circle the beast, near enough to touch him if she dared.

His thick fur collected snow like glitter. Her breath caught. Luc made a strikingly beautiful wolf.

Sam slowly gathered enough courage to reach out a hand. She could have sworn the wolf's—no, Luc's—expression encouraged her. Falling snowflakes frosted the outer edges of his coat, turning the pewter to silver.

She touched him. Even now, she felt the familiar tingle of recognition, of heat.

The fur felt soft and silky. Tangling her fingers in the undercoat, she scratched and caressed. The sound Luc made low in his throat was the exact one he'd made when they'd kissed earlier. A sound of want and need and longing.

Finally, she stepped away and waited, not sure what she should do next.

Lifting his muzzle, Luc tasted the breeze. He turned in a circle, tail flying. Once, twice, a third time.

The firefly sparklers returned, so numerous and intense that they obscured him from her sight. Sam rubbed her eyes, peering at the flickering lights, trying to figure out what they were made of.

"Magic and promises," Luc's voice said, and as she registered this, the fantastic curtain parted and he stood before her, naked and utterly magnificent.

Man, not wolf. Yet both.

And hers.

Not even allowing herself to acknowledge this thought, Sam moved forward.

He met her halfway, body to body, his mouth on hers, crushing, devouring. He didn't even try to hide his arousal; she felt the hard press of it against her belly.

When they broke apart, both breathing hard, he reached out his hand. Without a second thought she took it, and he scooped up his clothes and led her deeper into the forest, to a tall, granite wall where he showed her a small, hidden cave. While she waited, shivering, he padded around naked, inspecting the interior for safety.

She thought of their nice, warm and cozy motel room with its soft beds and clean, crisp sheets. She opened her mouth to tell him they should go there, but then he looked at her and she realized she couldn't.

Luc was still part animal; she saw a wild, ferocious hunger when she gazed into his eyes.

He came to her, his mouth searching, seeking. When he touched her, she felt warm again, and she allowed herself to melt into his heat, her own need rising to meet his.

Her clothes stood between them, an annoying barrier, and despite the snow and the cold, when they broke apart she helped Luc strip them from her body. When she, too, stood naked, totally exposed to him for the first time and shivering, he ran his hand down her side.

Where he touched, heat blazed. One arm under the small of her back, he lowered her to a bed of leaves, covering her body with his.

When he entered her, she cried out. He kissed her, again and again, with each stroke plunging deeper, his tongue matching his body. Never had lovemaking been like this, complete possession, utter abandon, *connecting*.

More than body, more than spirit, this was a juncture of souls.

As she reached for something she'd never been able to touch, the sky shattered and the snowstorm outside swirled. Her entire body vibrated, clenching him, cradling him, loving him. She cried out his name as she felt herself explode.

And the man she now knew she loved reached the same miraculous release, shuddering as he repeated her name over and over, his voice breaking.

She found herself wanting to weep.

Later, as they prepared to walk back to the motel in what appeared to have become a full-scale blizzard, she slipped her hand in his. Without his keen instincts for direction, she had no doubt they'd be lost, wandering the woods until they froze to death.

When they finally reached the motel, Sam shivered uncontrollably, chilled to the bone. Luc unlocked the door and pulled her into the warm room.

"Let's get you out of those wet clothes," he said, and proceeded to do just that.

Teeth chattering, she tried to help, but her shaking fingers refused to work.

Once she was naked again, he disrobed swiftly and yanked back the bedspread. "In here."

Too exhausted and cold to argue, she crawled beneath the sheets. He did the same, drawing her close.

Heat radiated off him.

"You're so warm." Snuggling into his warmth, she began to feel some of the chill leave her bones. "Why?"

Even without her elaborating, he understood the question. "One of the benefits of changing and then having fantastic sex. Now rest."

Closing her eyes, she let his warmth invade her once more, filling her in a different way than he'd done earlier. The steady beat of his powerful heart helped her drift off to sleep.

So far they hadn't noticed him. Never before had he prided his skill as a hunter. The ultimate prize—health and power—depended on catching them by surprise.

The other shifter had changed in front of Samantha.

He hadn't followed them too far into the woods,

*knowing the other's nose would be able to detect
him, no matter what steps he took to cover his
scent. He hadn't needed to follow, after all,
because he'd learned where the other was vul-
nerable, which fit perfectly with his plans.*

*Samantha and her remarkable power would be
his, and soon. Now he had only to implement his
plan.*

The snowplows came through early, clearing
the snow and salting the roads. The storm had
moved east, and when Luc checked the conditions
ahead of them, things didn't look good. Still, they
packed the car and checked out. They had no
choice but to try to reach Lucy.

More than anything, Sam wished she could
conquer her terror of flying. On this second day of
driving, she wondered if she looked as awful as she
felt. She hadn't dared glance in the mirror. Luc, on
the other hand, looked fantastic, as though he'd
just returned from a Caribbean vacation, energized
and cheerful. Being able to shape-shift into a wolf
appeared to have multiple benefits.

When they'd first heard the plows, Luc had
taken her into his arms. They'd made love again,

this time slow and lazily, with none of the desperate fierceness of the night before.

This time, when the tenderness overwhelmed her, she'd gotten out of bed and stepped into the shower.

By the time they'd both showered, the interstate heading east had been plowed, at least as far as Roanoke, Virginia. They'd take their chances, hoping the weather would improve by the time they reached that point.

But they encountered no real problems, other than low visibility and blowing snow.

After a brief stint in Maryland, they finally crossed into Pennsylvania. "We've got another eight hours or so, and that's with good road conditions," he warned. "We'll stop for lunch around Scranton. That's where we pick up I-84 and head east again."

Engrossed in reading the books he'd loaned her, she nodded. Every text had something definitive to say about healers.

She devoured them, marveling at the intricate details that had been recorded of each healer's life. They were always born Halflings, and the first indication of their talent had been their inability to change. They'd honed their abilities by performing healings on small animals, both wild and domestic, before entering the training to heal other

Halflings. This experience perfected their skills, but no one throughout the ages, from Pack scientists to Pack doctors, had ever been able to learn exactly *how* they healed.

Healers were considered blessed, right up there on a par with the saints Sam had learned about in catechism as a youth. Such a gift defied reason and logic, but then, so did the Packs' very existence.

With interest, Sam learned what she might be, and learned, too, of the limitations of her abilities. She could not heal anyone who did not want to live. She could not bring anyone back from the dead. And, most important, no one could force a healer to heal. In such an instance, the healer's ability would not make itself manifest.

By the time Luc and Sam stopped for lunch, she felt excited.

"I never knew," she told him, clutching one of the books while she munched on her cheese-and-steak sandwich. "All this time I had a purpose in life, and no one told me. So many years wasted."

Mouth full, he nodded, his gaze roaming over her face.

Once they were back on the road, she resumed reading. When she'd finishing poring over the last book, she closed the cover and grinned at Luc. "Thank you."

Glancing at her, he smiled back. "You're welcome."

Hours later, after they'd eaten supper at The Golden Arches and the sun had slipped to the edge of the horizon, they passed a sign welcoming them to New York State.

"Finally," Sam breathed, shifting in the seat and trying to ease the discomfort in her back.

"It's snowing again."

Sure enough, huge white flakes were drifting down.

"Once we get off the interstate, the roads won't be as well-maintained," Luc said. "Yet I'd hate to stop for the night when we're so close."

"It's not even dark." Sam leaned her head on his shoulder. She couldn't seem to stop touching him. "As long as this car can make it, I say we push on."

"We haven't got too much farther to go." Excitement made him sound boyish. When she glanced at him, he winked, and her apprehension lifted.

In the dusky light, the countryside was beautiful, even in mid-November when most of the leaves had fallen. She wondered why the landscape made her feel so secure; then she realized the snow-shrouded trees and softly rolling hills provided a sort of shield between the earth and the immense, slate-colored sky.

As night finally settled in, the falling snow and the hum of the tires on snow-covered pavement were lulling. Luc turned on the radio, scrolling through numerous country music stations until he located one playing top forty tunes.

"You know, getting used to this Pack thing isn't easy." Stretching, Sam tried to reposition herself in the seat to ease the growing ache in the small of her back.

"I can imagine. I also should warn you, once they find out you *are* a healer, your life will get a little crazy."

"Crazy how?"

Luc chuckled. "Healers are very rare. No one in my generation or my father's generation has known one. You'll be revered and loved, but I doubt you'll get a moment's peace until they get used to you."

She looked out the window while she mulled this over, knowing he needed to keep his attention on the road and the ever worsening weather conditions. Now the snow came down heavily, so thick they couldn't see past the beam of their headlights.

Worse, the window defroster wasn't working too well, making it even more difficult to see.

"Please keep talking to me. For some reason…" He hesitated, then gave her a wry smile. "For some reason, the sound of your voice soothes me."

"I was thinking about the crush of people you've described. And you know what?" Sam asked. "Maybe that won't be such a bad thing for me. I've been kind of lonely."

Until you came. Taking a ragged breath, she forced herself to continue. "I've been alone for a while, ever since my divorce. It might be nice to have more people around."

As long as Luc stayed by her side. The depth of her longing frightened her.

"How long were you married?"

"Four years." She wanted to say more, to steer the conversation back to banalities. Even though they'd talked about this before, the discussion suddenly seemed intensely personal. Too personal.

Yet Sam couldn't look away from Luc's profile.

Suddenly glad his driving occupied his attention, she chattered on about the potential adoption and decorating her nursery, pausing to catch her breath only when he reached over and wound a strand of her hair around his finger.

"I'm sorry," he said.

"Sorry I'm trying to adopt? Don't be. I know being a single parent is difficult, but I can do it."

"No, not that." The sidelong glances he sent her were smoldering ones, making her wish he would pull the car over and kiss her.

"I'm sorry your marriage ended."

A chill went through her. "And that I can't have children?" For a heartbeat or two, she allowed herself to savor his touch, before pulling away. Somehow, in the heady rush of physical attraction, she'd allowed herself to forget that no man would want her. Very few wanted a wife who couldn't give them offspring. She imagined someone like Luc would want several children, at least one boy and one girl.

The mental image caused Sam physical pain.

She realized he hadn't answered her question. No matter; he didn't have to. His response was written all over his handsome face.

"Don't be sorry. I'm not. I'm over it." She kept her voice flippant, unable to entirely hide her hurt. Time to change the subject. "What about you? Have you ever been married?"

"Once, a long time ago." He hadn't thought of Ana, his high school sweetheart and former wife, in years. "We married too young. It didn't work out."

Still smarting from the realization that she and Luc would never be more to each other, Sam decided to be honest. "Sometimes when I touch you, I sense a…chasm."

Her words shocked him, she could tell. Tightening his hands on the steering wheel, he swallowed hard. "Not from that marriage, believe me. That was over long before we divorced."

"Is the emptiness inside you because of your brother?" She voiced her question softly, to let him know she wouldn't pursue the subject if he wanted to drop it.

To her surprise, he gave a rueful nod. "I do want to talk about Kyle. I still miss him. He was only thirty-seven when the cancer took him."

Now it was her turn to reach out. "I'm sorry." She placed her hand on his arm and felt a rush of warmth, the awful ache in her throat easing somewhat. She could only hope her touch did the same thing for him.

"Kyle was my best friend and the glue that held our family together. After he died, my parents separated, even though Kyle was from a previous marriage of my mother's."

"Do your parents still live in Leaning Tree?"

"No. My father lives in Greece now, and my

mom moved to Vancouver. I'm the only one who visits Kyle's grave."

"He must have been pretty special."

Luc nodded. "He was. If he'd been a full-blooded shifter instead of a Halfling, he could have healed himself. If…" Luc's words trailed off, a muscle working in his jaw.

Another flash of clarity gave Sam the words to finish what he couldn't say. "If you'd had a healer then, Kyle would still be alive."

Luc didn't respond, though the guilt-stricken look on his face told her he'd suffered recriminations for this many times over.

"Full-blooded shifters like you—are you immortal then?"

"No. We age and die, just much more slowly than humans. And we can be killed, by silver bullets or fire."

"So that part of the legend is true."

"Yes. One advantage we do have is our resistance to sickness or injury. If we're hurt, we heal ten times faster than a human."

"But Ha-Halflings," she stumbled over the word, "don't."

"For minor things, like cuts and broken bones, they seem to have accelerated healing. Haven't you ever noticed this about yourself? Bruises go away in hours rather than days. Cuts seem to heal overnight."

"But major illnesses, like Kyle's cancer and Lucy's tumor, are barely slowed down?"

"Exactly."

"And you think I can heal these Halflings." Simply because she could heal small animals.

"Yes." Covering her hand with his, he lightly squeezed. "I do. After all, you healed Tomas."

"I hope you're right." She sighed. "Or there's going to be one big mess."

"I have faith in you."

She couldn't read the odd expression that flickered over his face when he said those words. Obviously, they meant something to him. What, she'd never know unless he told her.

"This is a lot to think about." More than he'd ever realize. Not only did Sam have to digest the possibility of a whole new aspect to the world, but she had to figure out how to put a damper on her feelings for him.

A semi blasted past them. Admiring Luc's competent driving, she watched as he kept their car from shimmying in the updraft.

"Someone's following us," he said a minute

later, his voice steady. "Don't look too obvious, but when you can, turn around. This snow makes it hard to tell, but I swear that looks like the maroon van from yesterday."

"The man who tried to grab me." Slowly, cautiously, she glanced over her shoulder. Even obscured by the swirling snowstorm, the vehicle right behind them appeared to be the one the stranger had driven.

As she watched, the van drew closer. "He's riding our bumper way too close for these conditions."

"He's been behind us for a good while, keeping up with us all along. Let's see what happens when I do this." Luc wrenched the wheel to the right, crossing two lanes to slide sideways down an exit ramp leading to a farm road.

Though he had to fight the steering wheel, he kept control of the car, making her admire his skill all the more. Impressed, Sam cheered when the dark-colored van had to stay on the freeway. A second later, it disappeared into the blizzard. "You lost him."

"For now." Luc shook his head. "Not for long, if that was the man who tried to grab you."

Sam clicked on the overhead light and unfolded the map. "I bet he's thinking he'll take the next exit and double back."

"Either that, or he'll drive on ahead to the first entrance ramp, pull over on the shoulder and wait for us. That's what I'd do. In order to avoid him, we'll keep going on the access road. The next town is about twenty miles ahead. With the way this snow is coming down, we need to find a place to stop for the night."

Blizzard conditions. Driving should have been easy, as Luc had lived all his life in the exceptionally wintry region of upstate New York. They crept forward, through snow coming down so hard and thick he could barely see twenty feet ahead. They were okay. Driving in this was doable, as long as no other drivers took unnecessary and foolish risks.

But black ice was an entirely different playing field. Luc never even saw the dark glaze under the lacy coating of powder.

As they went into a spin, he saw ahead the brake lights of the only other vehicle he'd spotted for miles. Too big for the van. Luc realized it was the Kenworth that had passed them earlier. The truck driver must have gotten off the freeway, too.

Why? Something clenched in Luc's gut. "Hell hounds!"

No time to question. He had to regain control of the car.

"What?" Sam took in the situation and stared straight ahead, jaw clenched as she clutched the door panel.

"Jackknifing semi. No way can we stay on the road and not hit it."

Still, he had to try. Steering into the spin, he pumped the brakes, even knowing it was useless. The car continued sliding forward, tires independent of the road.

"No traction?"

"Ice."

They continued the spin, heading directly toward the careening semi. At this speed, if they hit, there'd be nothing left of them but pieces.

Because he had no other choice, Luc yanked the steering wheel toward the right shoulder, off the road. He hadn't found his mate only to lose her.

On the shoulder, the tires finally grabbed. Regaining a semblance of control, Luc began the arduous process of steering them away from the Kenworth.

"Look out!" Sam screamed.

Bam. The maroon van appeared out of nowhere. It broadsided them, hitting hard and putting them into another spin. What little control Luc had was gone.

Ahead, the truck did a complete 180, sliding in slow motion directly toward them.

The van slammed into them again, this time on the passenger's side. They went careening across the median like a figure skater gone mad, spinning, spinning. Luc braked and jerked the steering wheel hard to the right once more.

If they could get off the road, they'd have a chance.

Chapter 10

Stomach plummeting as they barreled down the embankment, Luc managed to hang on to the wheel and keep the car from rolling. The vehicle shook as they plowed into a snowdrift. Earth and rock and trees and snow sent up a shower of white as they shuddered to a stop.

Eyes closed, Sam gripped the door. Her lips moved as though she was in prayer.

Any second now Luc expected to feel the impact of collision with either the truck or the van. At the speed both vehicles had been traveling, he feared they'd explode and burst into flame.

Instead, miraculously, when the car finally shuddered to a stop, the only sound left was the engine ticking.

From the passenger seat, Sam moaned, sending Luc's already rapid heartbeat into overtime.

"Are you hurt?"

"I don't think so." Expression dazed, she fumbled with the seat belt, trying to unlatch the buckle.

Relief flooded him, so intense he leaned over and planted a quick, hard kiss on her mouth. "Wait here," he said grimly, reaching to turn off the ignition, only to realize the engine had already died.

"Where are you going?" Glancing from him to the window, she shook her head. "Have you looked out there?"

The swirling snow was so thick and heavy they couldn't see the car hood in front of them.

Luc couldn't tear his gaze away from Sam. The entire incident made him feel as if he'd done battle for her. With adrenaline still pumping through his veins, he swallowed hard. "Unless you've come up with a better plan, I'm going to go for help. That jackknifed semi shouldn't be too far away. Those guys usually have CBs."

"Let me come with you."

"You don't have a coat," he pointed out. "Wait here. This shouldn't take that long."

Finally, she nodded. The forlorn look in her expressive eyes nearly made him change his mind, but he pushed open his door, blew her a kiss, then disappeared into the swirling snow.

Sam huddled in the car, an old blanket that she'd retrieved from the backseat wrapped snugly around her.

For a Texan used to a warm climate, this was torture. Yet she knew things could be worse—she and Luc could be dead or severely injured.

A tap on the window made her jump.

"Already?" she said, turning.

The masked face peering back at her wasn't Luc.

"What the—?"

The stranger yanked the door open, grabbing Sam by the elbow. Struggling, she saw a flash of metal as the intruder's arm swung back. A knife? Or something else, like another syringe?

This was the same man who'd grabbed her before. The one who'd called her a healer.

She wanted to fight him, but the blanket restricted her movements. With a hoarse cry, she shook it loose and shoved it at the masked man, attempting to wrap it around his head.

Her sudden move worked. The man stumbled, then fell to his knees in the snow, thrashing and grunting.

The blowing snow felt like pinpricks of ice hammering at her skin. She struggled to pull the door closed, with the crazy idea of locking it, since she wouldn't make it far in the blizzard without a coat.

But the locks had frozen and wouldn't work.

The masked stranger yanked off the blanket and came at her again.

This time, Sam didn't wait around. She'd take her chances with the cold and snow rather than face another hypodermic needle at the hands of some crazy man. Scrambling across the driver's seat, she opened that door, dived out and took off running in the direction Luc had gone, hoping against hope that she'd find him.

Behind her, she heard a shout.

Don't look back, don't look back.

"Sam?" Luc's voice. Close.

Relief flooding her, she screamed his name. He came running and met her halfway, his breath puffs of mist in the frigid air.

"What are you doing out here? I told you to wait

in—" They both heard the roar of an engine. A second later, the maroon van appeared, heading directly toward them.

"Come on." Grabbing her arm, Luc yanked her with him. "If we can make it to the truck, he can't hit us."

Though she could see it was likely a lost cause, Sam gamely struggled to keep alongside Luc.

Luckily for them, the van hit another icy patch and spun out.

With a sense of the miraculous, they kept going. The wrecked tractor-trailer rig loomed like a sunken ship in the blinding snow.

"Here," Luc grunted, swinging her around. "You're safe." He wrapped his coat around her shoulders.

They both tensed at the sound of the van's tires spinning, then the roar of its engine as it drove away.

Looking grim, Luc stared at the spot where the vehicle had vanished. "If we don't put a stop to this guy, he'll be back."

"He tried to grab me again." Sam fought to catch her breath. "Same guy, with a syringe. I don't know why he would try to run us over."

"Maybe he was trying to take *me* out. Obviously he thinks you can heal him."

"Why not just ask? From what you've told me, once we find out if I can heal Halflings, I'll be healing pretty regularly." She liked the sound of that. As though she'd been born for another purpose, one as far away from the simple pleasure she'd taken in helping people find books in the quiet town library.

"I don't know. Maybe he's planning to use you another way, like charge people to see you rather than have you heal for free."

"Speaking of healing, how is the truck driver?"

"He's all right. He's radioed for help. Tow trucks should be here soon." Luc took her arm. "Let's go wait in the cab with him. Your lips are turning blue."

An hour later, the wrecker dropped them off at Clem's Motor Lodge. A faded sign proclaimed American Owned and American Proud.

Though the motel parking lot was full, Luc hoped they could get a room. Many stranded travelers were bunking down for the night. Still, it didn't hurt to try.

With Sam swaying on her feet behind him, he asked for a room as far from the road as possible. When the clerk told him they had just one left, Luc handed over his credit card with relief. He was glad the unit was at the back of the building, near some trees and a snow-covered field.

Before the night was over, Luc suspected he would be making use of this proximity to nature. His one recent change hadn't been enough. Tension radiated in his blood, and his inner wolf paced within the confines of the human cage. When the blizzard ended and the moon rose in a star-studded sky, he knew he'd have to allow his wolf to run and hunt.

But when he got into bed beside Sam, intending only to hold her until she fell asleep, she curled into the curve of his body. Wrapping himself around her, he felt his tension ease. At peace, he slept.

At the sound of the snowplows in the morning, Sam opened her eyes and stretched. The tantalizing scent of the man lying beside her teased her nose. Intently conscious of his warm flesh touching her, she peeked through her lashes to see if he'd awakened.

He had. And he was watching her as intently as if he was committing every inch of her body to memory. The heat in his smoldering gaze and the tenderness in his expression intoxicated her, starting a slow burn inside.

"Come here."

She scooted over.

When he brushed a kiss on her shoulder and moved his lips to the hollow of her neck, she shuddered. He took her into his arms and kissed her with a softness that brought tears to her eyes. Though urgency mounted within her, he kept his ardor contained as he claimed her with his body. They made love, this time tantalizingly slowly, with nothing like the desperate fierceness of before. For some reason, this intensified the ache rather than easing it.

When he brought her to climax, she cried out his name. As her body clenched around him, he gave an answering cry as he went with her over the edge.

Afterward, he held her. Neither spoke. Sam struggled with the oddest urge to weep.

With Luc, she felt as if she'd come home. But she could never give him children, and a man like him deserved to have a son or daughter of his own.

Pushing herself out of the bed at long last, she went to the restroom and got dressed in the same clothing she'd worn the day before. The only clothing she had.

When she emerged, Luc was already dressed.

Luc checked the road conditions on his cell

phone. Storm conditions were reported all through the region, though nothing too severe.

After gobbling down waffles at the motel restaurant and fortifying themselves with hot coffee, they set out.

"We should be there in under an hour, if the road stays open."

They encountered no real problems, other than low visibility and blowing snow. The roads had been cleared and there were no black ice warnings.

Luc clicked on the radio and concentrated on his driving. They picked up I-87 heading north and went through New Paltz on the way to Kingston.

"Route 28 will take us up into the Catskills," he told Sam. "I wish there was more daylight left, so you could see the mountains."

"I'm sure I'll have time to see everything later." After she'd healed the little girl. Sam bit her lip. She could only hope there hadn't been some mistake, and her healing talent did extend to Halflings.

Halflings. She could scarcely believe she'd even thought it. Her nervousness grew in direct proportion to the distance from the town. The last sign had said twelve miles.

"You'll know we're getting close to Leaning

Tree when you start seeing old-time streetlights."
Luc reached over and squeezed her shoulder.
"Relax. Everything's going to be all right."

Easy for him to say. She concentrated on
watching for the streetlights.

"Look, there's one."

The lights were charming, made of black iron
with round, white globes, like old gaslights. Just
as Luc had promised.

"Here we are."

Welcome to Leaning Tree. Ringed by carefully
manicured shrubs, the brick sign looked well
maintained and very homey.

Sam tried to relax. As though he sensed her
tension, Luc began to massage her neck. His touch
felt so good, she let herself soften a fraction.

On the outskirts of town, small, wood-frame
houses nestled among the oaks and maples. As
Sam and Luc neared the center, the homes grew
larger and more ornate. Perfectly restored Victo-
rians in pastel shades looked welcoming and beautiful with the sun reflecting off the snow.

Awed, Sam could only stare. "I've never seen
anything like this before, at least in real life. Your
town looks like something out of a Christmas card."

His answering grin made her mouth go dry.

"Wait until you see downtown. After we make this curve, we'll be there."

Right away she tensed.

"Hey." His voice was tender. "I won't let anyone or anything hurt you."

Oddly enough, his words made her feel better.

"Here we are. Downtown Leaning Tree."

She gazed around, glad of the distraction. The storefronts were clean, painted to look brand-new. Various shops lined the tree-shaded street, including a root beer stand complete with carhops. People bustled in and out of stores, stopping to talk, shopping bags dangling from their hands.

"Rush hour in Leaning Tree," Luc quipped.

Enchanted, Sam gazed around in wonder. She felt as if she had stepped into an alternate reality. In a way, she had.

"I graduated from high school there." Luc pointed. Leaning Tree High, a three-story, faded brick building of the early 1900s, sat at the corner of Main Street and 12th. Wide granite steps curved wide around an elaborate doorway.

"It's beautiful. The entire place is magical—like a movie set in the fifties."

He grinned. "We're almost to Carson and Brenna's house. They live on the other side of town."

Swallowing nervously, Sam nodded. "In a Victorian like these?"

He shook his head. "The houses in that part of town aren't as old. I'm thinking they were built in the forties and fifties. Younger couples, like Carson and Brenna, have been buying them and restoring them."

Luc drove two more blocks, then turned right, stopping in front of a one-story bungalow painted a soft shade of cream. It sat back from the sidewalk on a wide, manicured lawn. Well-trimmed evergreen hedges surrounded the house.

"See those brick-edged flower beds?" He pointed. "In the spring, they're full of bright yellow daffodils and multicolored tulips. Brenna's sister-in-law, Lyssa, is legendary around here for her green thumb and she's helped Brenna learn to garden."

"It's beautiful," Sam breathed. "I can't even imagine how it would look with all the flowers. Absolutely gorgeous, I'll bet."

Luc took a deep breath. "Are you ready?" His excitement—and apprehension—felt palpable.

Her own stomach churning, Sam nodded, trying to smile. "I don't leave town much," she said, only half joking.

He came around to her side of the car and opened the door, helping her down. She squeezed his hand in thanks, for she still felt a bit battered and sore from the accident and the fight with the strange man.

Now here they were. She had a sense of coming head-to-head with her own destiny.

Taking her arm, Luc led her up the walkway. Before they'd gone two steps, the front door opened and a lean, blond man came out. Worry had carved lines in his craggy face and his dark eyes were full of pain. He took one look at the crumpled rental car and grimaced. "What the hell happened to you?"

"Alex." Luc moved ahead and clapped his arm around the other man's shoulders. "We got stuck in the blizzard and hit some black ice. Where's Carson?"

"He's at the hospital. Lyssa's there with him."

Sam noticed Luc didn't tell his friend about the stranger's attempt to grab her.

Luc drew her forward. "Alex Lupe, meet Sam Warren. Sam, this is my old high school buddy and one of my best friends."

Taking her hand, Alex smiled, but his eyes remained sad. "You must be the healer. My sister Brenna has been waiting for you. Welcome."

She winced. "I'm not sure—"

"Where she's going to stay," Luc interrupted,

warning her with a dark look not to voice her doubts. "Let's take a run by my place on the way to the hospital."

Alex looked from one to the other, his sharp gaze missing little. "You're welcome to stay here. Brenna and Carson have an extra room."

The chilly breeze made Sam shiver. Both men noticed.

"I'm from Texas," she said, only half-apologetically.

"Inside for you." Luc steered her toward the front porch.

As they climbed the steps, the front door opened again and a slender woman, her auburn hair in a long, fat braid down her back, stood poised in the doorway. Sleek and graceful, she brought to mind an exotic, well-groomed animal, though not a wolf. More like a gazelle or deer, Sam thought.

Her huge brown eyes and pale face made her look wraithlike, as though she hadn't slept in days. Most likely she hadn't.

Unsmiling, she came down the steps and held out her hand. "I'm Brenna. I'm so glad you could come." Her handshake was firm, but her skin was ice-cold.

"I'm Sam." Sam glanced at Luc, not sure what else to say.

"Come here, Brenna Turner." Luc enveloped the other woman in a tight embrace. "How are you holding up?"

She drew back, looking directly at Sam and ignoring the question. "If you don't mind, I'd like to go to the hospital now. I want you to heal my baby."

Throat tight, Sam nodded. "Of course." She prayed Luc was right and that her gift would work with this little girl.

"Excellent. Are you ready then?"

"If you don't mind, I'd like to use your washroom first to freshen up." Sam dragged her hand through her hair. "We've been in the car for two days."

Expression wooden, Brenna stared at her. "My child is dying. I only left her side to come greet you with the respect accorded a healer."

"I don't even know if I—" Sam began.

This time Luc's hand on her arm stopped her. "Don't."

Brenna's face crumpled and she turned away, shoulders shaking as she began to cry.

Immediately, Alex went to her, pulling the weeping woman to his chest. "She's been through a lot," he told them.

Sam nodded. What had she gotten herself into? What if she couldn't heal their little girl? What then? She didn't suppose Luc had thought of that.

"I think we both could use the washroom," Luc murmured.

"Of course." Alex started toward the house, keeping his arm around his sister's shoulders. "Let me show you where it is."

They filed into the bungalow. Sam resisted the urge to look at Brenna, to offer the woman some small comfort. How could she, when for all she knew her very presence brought false hope?

Despite the spacious size, the guest bathroom, decorated in peach and white, had a cozy feel. The marble counters and fixtures sparkled and the ceramic tile floor gleamed. As Sam washed her face, she heard the murmur of the others' voices as they talked.

While she hoped she could heal Lucy, she couldn't help but picture the disappointment and pain a failure would bring this family. How could she live with herself if she failed?

After blotting her face with a towel, Sam squared her shoulders. Knowing she had Luc by her side, even if only temporarily, gave her some small comfort. To imagine a future without him was to picture an existence so desolate she couldn't bear to think about it.

Opening the door, she pasted on what she hoped was a confident look, and stepped out to face Lucy's parents.

The drive into New York City took longer than she'd expected. Still, riding in the backseat of Alex's SUV, she snuggled into Luc's side and tried to settle her nerves by thinking carnal thoughts. But when Luc's breathing quickened as though he could read her mind, she realized she wanted nothing more than to fling open the back door and leap from the moving vehicle.

"Relax." He spoke close to her ear. "Everything is going to be all right now."

"Easy for you to say," she whispered back. "What if—"

He silenced her the only way that could have— by kissing her.

She pressed into him, grateful at first for the distraction. But as he deepened the kiss, plundering her mouth as though he couldn't get enough, she forgot everything but the feel of the strong man holding her in his arms.

"Ahem." Alex cleared his throat, making her jump guiltily. Flushing as she met his gaze in the rearview mirror, Sam smoothed her hair and looked everywhere but at Luc.

In the front seat, Brenna turned to glance at them curiously, apparently unaware anything had been going on.

Winking at Sam, Luc shifted, crossing his legs to hide his arousal.

They rode the rest of the way in silence, Luc's fingers threaded through hers, his closeness banishing the trepidation from her heart.

About an hour into the drive, Brenna's cell phone rang. She glanced at the caller ID and blanched. "The hospital."

Everyone listened tensely while she spoke a few words into the receiver. "I understand." Her voice broke as she concluded the call.

When she turned to look at Alex, her eyes were full of tears. "She's fading fast. Her vital signs are dropping and Carson said Dr. Nettles doesn't think she'll last the night."

Alex jerked his head in a nod and pressed the accelerator to the floor, swinging into the fast lane and staying there until they reached the outskirts of the city and traffic slowed their frenetic rush.

"Carson and Lyssa are keeping a vigil," Alex

said, when they finally arrived at the hospital and swung into the parking garage.

Brenna nodded, her tight expression reflecting her worry. She drummed her long fingernails on the dashboard, her agitation palpable.

Sam's stomach hurt as her own worry grew. She could only hope they weren't too late. Worse, what if this didn't work? Who was she, Samantha Warren, to let them believe she could heal their beautiful, gravely ill daughter, when she had no idea if she truly could?

"You can," Luc told her, raising her chin to make her look at him. "Believe in yourself."

"How do you do that?" Sam pulled away, glaring at him. "You keep answering questions that are inside my head."

Luc opened his mouth, closed it and then shrugged. "I don't know."

Without turning around, Brenna answered, "Sometimes we can tell what our mate is thinking. That's one of the benefits of mating for life."

Mate?

"I'm no one's mate," Sam answered firmly. A woman who couldn't have children could never be a mate to a man like Luc.

Beside her, he stiffened.

Pulling into an empty space, Alex parked. Brenna jumped out before Sam had even unfastened her seat belt. Sam could forgive the impatience radiating from the other woman. She knew if her own child lay dying, she'd be hurrying to bring salvation, too.

Luc took Sam's arm as they fell into step behind Alex and Brenna. "When this is over, we'll talk," he told her.

Heart heavy, she nodded. Every footstep echoing on the pavement seemed to be telling her she was a fool. If modern medicine couldn't help Lucy...

"You will," Luc said.

Sam glared at him.

Inside the hospital, they took the elevator up to Lucy's room.

"There are only thirty-eight beds in the pediatric oncology department," Alex said. "We were very lucky to get one for her."

Brenna glanced at them, her expression bleak. "But even with eighteen oncologists on staff, they said they couldn't help Lucy." She grimaced. Then, visibly collecting herself, she took a deep breath. "I so hope you can perform a miracle."

A miracle. Sam wanted to hang her head. Only

the touch of Luc's hand at the small of her back kept her from doing so. She'd tried to tell him she wasn't a miracle worker, but he wouldn't listen.

A dying little girl, even if she was half shifter, was a giant leap from a wounded puppy or kitten.

The elevator doors opened. Brenna and Alex got out and headed to the left. Sam wanted to hang back, but Luc propelled her forward.

She exited the elevator in time to see Brenna and Alex enter a room up the hall.

"Come on. Everything will be all right." Luc took Sam's hand, tugging her gently along the corridor.

As they passed, another door opened.

A man stepped out. He grabbed Sam, jerking her away from Luc and pushing her into the room. Then he slammed the door in Luc's face.

Chapter 11

Stumbling, Sam fell and narrowly missed hitting her head on the TV stand. Pushing herself to her feet, she faced her assailant.

"You." He was the same guy who'd tried to grab her twice before, though this time, she noted, he didn't have a syringe. Thank God.

He'd jammed a chair under the knob. Despite Luc's furious efforts, the door wouldn't open.

"Buying time," the man said, cocking his head. "So you remember me?"

"How could I forget?" She stared at him, puzzled. "How did you know to come here?"

He held up a metal box. "The miracles of modern technology. I bugged Patricia's phone. Once I knew where you were going—Sloan-Kettering in New York—it was easy to keep track of you. I learned where the little Halfling girl is, and with a stolen orderly uniform, all I had to do was wait."

"Why are you doing this? What do you want with me?"

He smiled, showing yellowing teeth. "What does everyone want with you? Healing, of course. Do you really think these people would give you the time of day if they couldn't use you?"

His casual cruelty hurt, though she took care not to show it. "They won't let you get away with this."

As if on cue, the door bulged as Luc hurled himself against it. He roared with rage when it didn't budge.

Again he slammed into it. The chair held.

"We don't have much time. Heal me now," the man demanded, his eyes wild. "Before your mate breaks down the door."

Which would be any minute, judging from Luc's furious attempts.

Stall for time.

"Who are you?" she asked. "I don't even know your name."

"You *don't* remember me?"

She cocked her head. "Other than the two times you've attacked me, I've never seen you before."

"You've forgotten then. You knew me once." His mouth twisted. "When we were small."

Searching her memory, she drew a blank. "I don't—"

"Try. Think back to when you were two."

Something…some memory, long forgotten, teased the back of her mind.

Luc slammed against the door again, causing the man to jump.

"Tell me your name," Sam demanded.

"I'm Michael."

"Michael?" The name, too, struck a chord, though she had no idea why. "I don't know anyone named Michael."

"You know me. You've always known me, even if we haven't seen each other in thirty years."

Outside in the hall, she could hear the sound of Luc conferring with Carson and someone else. From the wary look on Michael's face, he heard them, too.

"Stop the games," she told him. "And tell me who you are."

"I'm your brother."

A suffocating sensation clogged her throat. "I don't have a brother," she whispered.

Bam. Luc and reinforcements slammed against the door. Hard. Judging from the sound, Carson and the other man had joined him.

"Don't say that! Of course you have a brother."

"No, I—"

"You don't remember me." Michael's voice shook—Sam couldn't tell if it was with rage or grief.

Was it possible he *was* really her brother?

She chose her words carefully. "How could I? I don't even remember my father."

"You're lucky." His expression bleak, Michael began to pace. The restless energy in his movements reminded her of Luc. "Though a lot of people thought he was brilliant, I know better. He was insane."

Swallowing, she tried to understand. "I don't—"

"Our parents were selfish. They cared only for themselves. Our mother wanted you because you were human. But me…"

Sam could understand his pain. All her life she'd felt similar echoes whenever she wondered why her own father didn't love her.

Again the men rammed the door. Still, the chair and the thick wood held.

"All my life, Father told me how you were destined for a life of greatness, while I...was nothing."

"He *knew?*" Her voice rose. "Are you saying he knew I might be a healer, and still he left me to be raised completely ignorant?"

Michael nodded. "It's possible. I told you he was nuts. In his own way, he hated the Pack. Even though he returned to live among them, he did everything he could to prevent them learning about you. He never knew for sure if you were really a healer."

"He didn't bother to try and find out."

"I know."

"But why?"

He lifted his hands in a shrugging gesture. "Who knows?"

The sounds from outside the door had stopped. Sam knew Luc wouldn't have given up and gone away. More likely, he'd regrouped with Alex and Carson and was coming up with a better plan.

"I still don't understand. Why separate siblings? Mother hated my father. She had so much bitterness, it was painful to see. But you—you're her child. You had nothing to do with any of that."

Expressionless, he watched her. "Evidently she

felt I did. Father was the same way. Lonely and re-sentful. He never stopped hating her for making him leave. I think he truly believed she was his mate. When she didn't want him, he couldn't make himself strip her of the only one she loved—you."

They'd each lived with the crippling knowl-edge, trying to fathom how a parent could abandon their own child.

"Maybe in her own way, she loved you."

His mouth turned down. "How could you think she did? She cut me completely from her life. She never called, never sent a birthday card, and didn't even tell her baby daughter—you—that I existed. What kind of mother does that? She simply turned her back on me and acted as though I'd never been born."

Sam didn't know what to say. His hurt was so visible, so similar to her own, that she wanted to hug him. But he'd kidnapped her, was trying to force her to heal him, and she still didn't know for sure he was who he claimed to be.

"All we have is each other," Michael said.

Sam bit her lip and said nothing. In one way, he was right—she had no family that she knew of, except for him.

If he was telling the truth. Studying his face, she saw no hint of her mother's features or her own.

"You still doubt me?" he asked. Before she could answer, he reached into his shirt pocket and pulled out a black-and-white photo. Passing it to her, he waited.

At first, she couldn't comprehend. The faded picture showed a man, a woman Sam recognized as her mother in younger days, and two small toddlers, arms linked. One was Sam. The other…

"Me," he said quietly. "Our family, in happier times, though this disease has made me look like an old man."

Suddenly, anger filled her. "If you knew, why did you do things this way?" she asked. "Why not simply come to me and tell me? Why use force?"

The regret vanished from his face. "Because our father trained me well. He had a plan, and made sure I could implement it before he died. I am strong, a good hunter, but once your abilities are known you will have all the power. You'll be honored and revered by our people. *My* people. Meanwhile, I'm…"

"Sick?"

"Dying," he snapped. "I'm dying, Samantha."

"Not tonight." Handing back the photo, she kept

her voice gentle. "You aren't dying right this instant, like Lucy."

Though he curled his lips into a snarl, he did not contradict her.

"I'm here to try to heal a dying little girl. She'd been given a week to live, but now they say she won't last out the night. If you let me go and heal her, I give you my word I'll heal you in a day or two."

"No. I don't want this cancer inside me. You'll heal me now. Once I'm well, I'll allow you to heal the sick kid. For a price."

Desperately, she tried to think of an explanation that would convince him. This man—Michael, her brother—obviously cared nothing about anyone but himself.

The door splintered, and burst open with a crash.

Michael cursed. Moving so fast Sam couldn't react, he spun and grabbed her. "I'm sorry it's come to this," he growled, holding a knife to her throat. "Heal me or die."

Luc and Alex froze. Behind them, a dark-haired man who could only be Carson stared.

"Sam." Luc started toward her.

Michael tightened his grip. "Don't come any closer," he warned. "Or she's dead."

Alex clamped his hand on Luc's shoulder.

"Calm down, man. More than Lucy's life is in danger now—Sam's is also at stake."

His eyes glowing with fury, Luc nodded. Carson let go of him, glaring at Michael. "What do you want?"

"Healing," Michael said. "And you two need to back off. This is between me and her."

Luc made a strangled sound.

"Blood to blood," Michael added.

"This defeats the purpose. If you kill her, you'll have no chance of being healed." Speaking in a calm, rational voice, Alex took a step in front of Luc, effectively blocking him. He also, Sam noticed, moved closer.

Michael laughed, a bitter, hollow sound. "I know that. If you two could have left well enough alone, I wouldn't have had to go this far. But my sister and I have some catching up to do."

"Sister?" Luc raised a brow.

Brenna appeared in the doorway. "What's going on?" Her eyes narrowed as she took in the situation, and she began backing away. "One of the nurses has called security."

"Keep them away or Samantha dies."

"But…" She glanced helplessly at Carson. "My little girl is…"

"Without this healer, she's already dead."

"Enough," Luc roared. Shoving aside Alex, he dived for Michael.

"No!" Carson twisted to grab him. Off balance, he only succeeded in knocking Luc sideways, slamming his head into the corner of the night-stand. Luc lay crumpled in a heap.

"Luc," Sam cried.

"Don't move." Michael still held the knife. "He's only stunned. He's a full-blooded shifter. Only fire or a silver bullet can kill him."

With a wolflike snarl, Brenna launched herself at him. Carson threw himself in her way, blocking her, holding her wrists as she raged.

This distraction enabled Luc to push himself up unnoticed. Having the same idea, Sam raised her arm, knocking the knife away from her throat at the same time Luc leaped for Michael.

The blade bit into Luc's neck.

Everyone, including Sam, froze.

"Luc!" Brenna gasped. "Hell hounds, he's—"

"Don't move." Taking advantage of the situation, Michael twisted the knife. Blood trickled from the deeper wound. "Any of you."

Sam couldn't breathe. Couldn't think, couldn't

move. For the first time she understood the true meaning of the word *mate*. "Don't you hurt him."

"Heal me," Michael demanded, cutting his eyes to Sam. "If you want this man to live, heal me."

"A knife can't kill me," Luc managed to gasp. "Don't listen to him."

The other man laughed. "Fool." Using his other hand, he pulled out a small, chrome-plated pistol and pressed it against Luc's temple. "This is fitted with a silencer and loaded with silver bullets, which definitely will kill you. Make the smallest move and I'll squeeze the trigger."

Luc smiled, a cold, feral grin. A warning, Sam knew.

"Heal me, healer," Michael said, apparently choosing to disregard it. He made a movement, causing a thin ribbon of blood to leak from the wound and run down Luc's neck.

Sam's answering cry of rage was met with a smirk.

"This may not kill him, but it'll make him suffer like hell. He'll be pleading for that silver bullet before this is over. Now heal me."

She tried to reason with him once more. "Michael, there's a little girl down the hall. She's dying. Now. Tonight. Let me heal her first, then I'll heal you tomorrow."

"No. Me first."

"But she has no time. She's—"

"Now!" he roared. "Before I lose patience and your mate dies."

"I'll do it," she said, lifting her chin. "I give you my word."

"Sam," Luc protested. "Lucy—"

"Will be next." She cut him off. "Let me do this."

No one but him knew what two healings would do to her, especially ones much more complex than sick animals.

"I won't let you die," Luc vowed.

"Shut up." Michael ground his teeth. "She's already given me her word. Maybe I'll just kill you now and get it over with."

"You can't force a healer to heal."

"I'm not forcing her," Michael said. "She's given me her word. She wants to heal me, don't you, Samantha?"

Swallowing hard, Sam nodded.

Eyes glittering with rage, Luc fell silent. Sam knew he was weighing his options. Surely he realized if he tried to stop her from healing Michael, he'd die and be unable to prevent anything.

She read his decision in his face. He had no choice but to stand back and watch her heal them both.

. And pray she didn't die.

In the doorway, Brenna and Carson moved closer together, silently watching.

Sam took a deep breath. "I don't even know if this will work," she told Michael, ignoring Brenna's gasp. "I've only healed animals."

He bared his teeth, looking more like a wolf than a man. "I'm half animal. Now do your thing."

She barely hid a shudder of revulsion. "I have to touch you. Under your shirt." Hesitantly, she held out her hands, moving the cloth away and placing her fingers on the bare skin of his side.

Heal. Heat flared through her into him. Michael made a sound of wonder and of ecstasy.

As always happened, Sam saw flashes of his life. This time, rather than the disjointed impressions she received from animals, she saw clearly his life with their father, a stern man whose face looked totally unfamiliar, and others of his Pack.

"Sam." Luc was calling her name. She broke the trance to open her eyes, and saw him reaching out to touch her.

Michael growled, shifting his hand so the knife twisted in Luc's throat. Pain flashed across Luc's face, making Sam's heart stutter. Though the healing process shouldn't be interrupted, for Luc she'd risk anything. Even her life.

"Leave him alone," she cried, lifting her too-hot hands off Michael. "Or I won't finish."

All of them stared at her. Carson and Brenna wore identical quizzical and worried expressions, no doubt wondering if she could heal Michael. Luc watched her with tenderness and fear warring in his face.

And Michael...Michael watched her with greed.

He wanted more. More heat, more healing, more power.

She gave him all she had, healing him and knowing what would happen once he was whole. Every animal she'd ever healed fell unconscious when her gift started to work.

Michael was no different. Collapsing, he dropped the gun. It went off, shattering the television. At the same time, he pulled the knife free from Luc's throat.

Blood gushed. More blood than Sam had ever seen in her life.

"Luc!" she cried, running to him and instinctively placing her hands on his throat. She gave what little she had left, forgetting his life was not in danger, and refusing to let him suffer.

"No." He shoved her away. "Save Lucy," he managed to gasp, before collapsing again.

"He's right." Brenna took her arm, pleading with her eyes. "We shifters can heal ourselves."

Dazed, barely able to lift her head, Sam looked around the room. For the first time she noticed Carson was gone. "Where is he?"

"He had to go distract a curious nurse. She heard the noise and wanted to investigate." Brenna touched Sam's arm. "Please come and heal my daughter."

Sam inhaled and nodded. Holding on to Brenna's arm for support, she allowed the other woman to lead her out of the room and down the hall.

Luc must have blacked out. When he opened his eyes, he was alone in the room with a still unconscious Michael. Sam's brother. Whoever had gathered the intelligence on her had missed that one little detail.

Sam!

Pushing himself to his feet, he realized where everyone had gone. To Lucy's room. The Turners didn't know that Sam's powers were limited.

Heart thudding hard in his chest, he staggered into the hall, hoping against hope he'd make it in

time to stop her from trying to heal Lucy.
Somehow, some way, the doctors would have to
make the little girl hold on until tomorrow. Sam
couldn't heal her now—she'd die.

Slowly, he pulled the door open. It creaked,
causing Alex to turn. He beckoned Luc inside.
Sam was already kneeling by the bed. Brenna
stood at her side, head bowed, Carson clasping
her hand. Alex's wife, Lyssa, watched them, her
pretty face wearing a grave expression. An older
man with a full head of steel-gray hair, whose
scent told Luc that he was a shifter, kept a vigil at
the foot of the bed. He must be Dr. Nettles.

And Sam... In an instant, Luc realized Sam had
already placed her hands on Lucy's chest. Energy
pulsed in the room, so strong and intense that it
reminded him of how he felt when he changed
and became wolf.

Damn. Lucy looked so tiny, so helpless,
dwarfed by the large hospital bed. And Brenna—
beautiful, kind Brenna, wore an expression of such
hope she appeared transformed.

How could he stop this? He couldn't.

Yet he knew he couldn't lose Sam.

Quietly, he moved closer. Neither Brenna nor
Sam acknowledged his presence, though Carson

gave him a small nod. Under Sam's hands, the little girl took shallow breaths, her chest rising and then appearing to collapse. Lucy looked so wan and lifeless, so different from the bright, vibrant child he remembered.

Could Sam heal her? And if she did, would she be sacrificing her own life for Lucy's?

Frozen, Luc found himself praying for the first time since his brother died.

All he could think about was Sam's narrow brush with death after healing both the cat and the poodle. She knew the risks, yet still was willing to try to heal the three-year-old after curing her own long-lost, deranged brother.

Luc took a deep breath. God, how he loved her.

His throat aching, he stared at the tableau by the hospital bed, watching Sam and Lucy, uncertain what would happen to either of them if he interrupted now.

Radiating from the little girl, the heat and pressure and sense of power increased, constricting Luc's throat, his chest. What was this? In all his research on healers, he hadn't come across this. It was something new and different. A quick glance at the others told him they felt it, too.

Head bowed in prayer, Brenna moaned, an echo

of sound so low and otherworldly it sent a shiver down Luc's spine. Not quite a howl, closer to a cry.

A moment later, Alex tipped his head back and joined in. Not an expression of mourning, or even despair, but of hope and unity.

Of Pack.

Luc felt an answering cry building in him. The noise escaped him—almost as if pulled from his throat.

Only the humans, Carson and Lyssa, were silent, watching the shifters with wide eyes. The humans—and Sam. Head bent, the Halfling who could not change used her energy to heal.

While Luc watched, Lucy's pale skin became flushed. Faint at first, the color spread from her chest, slowly infusing her with rose. With health.

Brenna gave a glad cry and they all crowded around the bed, touching one another, drawing on each other's strength.

So intent were they on Lucy's returning health, none of them noticed Sam growing paler, blood-less, as though the healing process stole every ounce of her vitality. As if she were giving her own life force to the sick little girl.

Now Luc finally understood why healing drained her.

The monitors hooked to the little girl started going crazy. The doctor quickly punched some buttons, quieting the sound.

"Mama?" Lucy opened her eyes. Bright, curious eyes the color of a robin's egg, full of curiosity and health.

"Right here, sweetheart." With a glad cry, Brenna gathered her close. Carson put his arms around them both, unabashedly weeping.

Lucy smiled dreamily before her eyes drifted closed again.

And Sam slid to the floor. Unconscious.

Chapter 12

No! Rushing to Sam, Luc fell on his knees and gathered her in his arms.

The entire room went silent. Dr. Nettles came to her side. Taking her wrist, he felt for a pulse. "I'm sorry," he said, looking at Luc with stark pity in his gaze. "There's nothing I can do. She's gone."

Brenna and her brother, Alex, exchanged a long glance. "Our healer..." she said.

Luc shook his head. "She's not gone," he told them, his voice fierce, his heart thudding hard in his chest. "She's not."

This time, he saw sympathy in every one of their faces.

Except Samantha's. Her beautiful features wore no expression, no expression at all.

"Sam," he murmured. He felt…broken, as if what remained of his heart had been ripped away. "Sam, please."

She looked peaceful. As still as…

No.

Not Sam. He refused to believe she was dead. They'd only just found each other. He couldn't believe fate would so cruelly rip them apart before they'd even begun their life of love and happiness together. He'd helped her before, somehow. Maybe, just maybe, he could help her again.

"Luc, I'm sorry." Alex crouched by him and slung his arm around his shoulders in a gesture meant to comfort.

Luc wanted no part of it.

"Does that always happen when a healer heals?" Lyssa sounded hopeful, as if by her words she could bring a sense of normalcy back to the room.

"Only when—" His voice broke. "She does too much. She can't heal twice in one day. The last time she tried, her heart stopped. I got her to a hospital and they couldn't save her. She nearly died."

Nearly being the operative word. She'd somehow come back from the dead and woken in his arms.

He willed it to be so again.

"What happened then?" Carson asked, his expression expectant. "What did they do to bring her back?"

The others surrounded him, watching, solemn and quiet, the air of celebration gone. Little Lucy slept, a natural, healthy sleep, and though Brenna would not let go of her daughter's hand, she watched Luc and Sam with concern and expectation in her face.

Mutely, Luc stared at them, dimly aware of tears coursing down his cheeks.

"They must have done something," Lyssa said. "Maybe we can try the same thing now."

"Can we help? What can we do?" Carson and Alex, Lyssa and Brenna—Luc saw in their faces that they'd all help if they could.

"I don't know." Feeling more helpless than he had in his entire life, Luc gathered her lifeless body in his arms and kissed her lips. Maybe this was the secret cure. The last time he'd done it, she'd begun to breathe again.

Not so this time.

Suddenly, he realized what was wrong. This time, his energy alone was not enough.

"I do need your help. Please, make a circle around us. Touch me, help me, lend me your strength. We can bring her back."

Instantly, they did as he asked. Brenna let go of her daughter's hand to join them. Crouching on the floor around him and Sam, they linked hands and closed their eyes. He felt their unity, their love, their distress.

Pack.

Humans and shifters alike, they silently began to pray.

Sam still lay unmoving in Luc's arms.

Cradling her, rocking her gently, he felt Alex's palm on one shoulder. A second later, Brenna placed her hand on the other.

"Healer, heal yourself." Joining them, Dr. Nettles spoke the same words Luc had thought the last time Sam had fallen.

"Sam, heal. Don't leave me." Luc brushed a kiss against her cheek. When he lifted his head, her face was wet with his tears. "Sam, come back to me."

She didn't move.

"You're my mate," he said, ignoring Brenna's surprised gasp. "The other half of my soul."

He kissed her again. Then again, willing her to live.

And then her pale skin went from a frosty shade of ice to cream, flushing peach as her blood flow returned. Her chest rose as she took a shuddering breath, and then rose again.

"Ninety-five seconds," the doctor said. "Reviving now, she shouldn't suffer any neurological damage."

The others gave a quiet cheer.

Luc laughed. Joy flooded him. Not tentative, but strong and sure.

He kissed her again. Her lips curved in a dreamy smile. Holding her, he gave her his heart, his strength, his soul.

In return, she gave him healing. Opening her caramel-colored eyes, she connected her gaze with his, and he knew. Even now, weakened and near death, she was trying to heal. Him. She wanted to heal the rift that had festered so long in his soul.

"Stop," he told her, whispering against her lips. "Conserve your strength. You've already repaired what was wrong inside me, with your love."

Sighing, she kissed him. Weakly at first, but as he deepened the kiss, she responded with increased vigor.

"Ahem." Alex and Lyssa, Carson and Brenna all cleared their throats at once. "You two, there's a child present."

Blushing, Sam broke away. Brow wrinkled in confusion, she scrambled out of Luc's arms and tried to stand.

With his help, she was able to regain her feet.

"What happened?" Still shaky, she looked from one face to another, finally peering intently at the sleeping little girl. "Was I too late?"

When they told her she hadn't been, she nodded with satisfaction. "Good."

"*Very* good." Luc pulled her close, drinking in her scent, gazing at her and letting every emotion show in his eyes.

He knew the instant she realized. "You've been crying," she said in wonder, brushing his cheeks with her fingers. "I'm so, so sorry."

"Don't be. You healed them both."

She took a deep breath. "Though I'm still weak, I feel stronger. Again, you healed me."

"No," he corrected. "We all healed you. Together."

She smiled up at him, contentment shining in her face. Contentment and something else, something more.

Love. He could scarcely believe it.

"I love you, Luc," she told him, in case he had any doubt.

With a glad growl, he covered her mouth with his. "I love you, too."

"Mates," Brenna said, satisfaction ringing in her voice.

"Mates," Luc echoed, against Sam's lips.

At the word, Sam stiffened, pulling away. "I can't be your mate," she said. "You know I can't have children."

As Luc opened his mouth to tell her it didn't matter, Dr. Nettles came forward and placed his hand on her shoulder. "Have you been tested?"

"Yes."

The single word broke Luc's heart. He opened his mouth to tell her that didn't matter, but a sharp glance from the doctor stopped him.

"Were you trying to conceive with a human?" Dr. Nettles asked.

Sam nodded. "My ex-husband."

"That's the problem, then. You're a Halfling, and a special one at that. Some Halflings can only conceive with a full-blooded shifter. I think if you and your mate—" he glanced at Luc "—try to conceive, you'll be pleasantly surprised."

Tentative hope bloomed in Sam's eyes. "Really?"

The doctor smiled. "Yes, really."

With a glad cry, she flung herself at Luc, squeezing him tightly. Her joy was contagious, for everyone began to clap.

Luc kissed her instead.

Though the Anniversary police department was small, they had a working jail. One of the three cells held Michael. He'd been arrested on charges of kidnapping and aggravated assault.

Luc hadn't wanted Sam to visit him. But she'd insisted, explaining that having a brother felt too new and welcome for her to ignore.

"Even after what he did to you?"

She nodded. "Even so. I think his illness made him a little crazy."

Luc decided to let the "little" part pass. "I'm coming with you," he announced, unwilling to risk her to a known threat.

"Of course you are. He's your brother-in-law now."

Luc grimaced. "He also tried to hurt you."

"But he's healed," she reminded him. "He got what he wanted. He won't harm me now."

"You're forgetting his little comment about

power. He wanted to control you, so he could be in charge of who you healed."

She shook her head and didn't reply.

Once they arrived at the jail, Sam gripped Luc's hand tightly as they walked toward the holding area. She'd pressed charges, but had been wavering about withdrawing them. Luc knew that the FBI had gotten involved, since the kidnapping attempt had crossed state lines, and she'd be told she couldn't withdraw. That would likely upset her to no end, as she wouldn't want her newfound brother in a federal penitentiary.

Luc didn't feel nearly as benevolent.

Michael had been told to expect them, and already waited in the holding room. He smiled at them as Sam and Luc took their seats.

"I'd like to apologize," he said at once.

Luc watched Sam melt. "That's all right," she answered. "I completely understand."

"I don't," Luc growled. Sam squeezed his hand.

Michael ignored him, looking only at his sister. "You've given me my health. That means more to me than anything."

Luc refrained from saying he was glad Michael would get to enjoy his health while he served time in prison for kidnapping—and the murder of their father. He'd confessed to setting the fire and ending his father's life.

Sam took a deep breath. "I had a reason for wanting to talk to you."

At Michael's expectant look, she shook her head. "Not the reason you're thinking. I want to know if we—I—have any living relatives in the Pack where you and our father lived in Maine."

"Of course we do. There's Aunt Merriam and Uncle Ben, and scores of cousins. Why, if you drop the charges against me, I'll personally introduce you."

Still holding Luc's hand, Sam rose. "That won't be necessary. Luc and I will pay them a visit. I'm sure we can find everyone."

"But what about the charges?"

Sam stiffened. "What do you mean? You've confessed to everything. They're not going to let you go."

"I know that." Expression serious, he cocked his head and looked at her. "But I meant you. Do you think you will ever forgive me?"

Because there had been so many lies already, he deserved the truth. "I don't know," she whispered, her eyes filling with tears. "There's so much I have to think about."

"Once you come to terms with everything?" Hope shone in his face. "Maybe?"

She could promise nothing, but she was going to try to adjust—and maybe even forgive. Just not yet. It was too soon. "Maybe," she managed to say. "One day."

On the way out the door, Sam looked over her shoulder. "Good luck, Michael. Write me and let me know where you end up, and I'll write back."

Once they were in the car, she started crying. "That was the hardest thing I've ever done."

Luc kissed her cheek.

"You'll make a damn good mother," he said gruffly, and started the car.

Nine months later

Waddling into the coffee shop, Sam smiled. She'd arrived before either Jewel or Patricia, which meant they could sit at the bar. Patricia preferred a table, but she was the only one with a normal size stomach.

Climbing aboard the bar stool was no easy feat, given Sam's size. Eight months and three weeks pregnant, and deliriously happy, she felt as if she might pop at any second.

The bells over the door jingled. Since Jewel

was carrying twins, her stomach arrived before she did. Patricia hurried along behind, looking tiny in comparison.

Sam waved at them.

"No way can I sit at the bar," Jewel said. "Let's take a booth."

"I doubt you could fit in a booth, either," Sam teased. "Your size is sooo impressive. I'm jealous."

"Don't be." Rubbing the small of her back, Jewel grimaced. "The little twerps won't let me sleep. Worse, when I glance in the mirror I look like a huge swine about to have a litter."

Sam laughed. "No you don't. You look like a very pregnant, very beautiful woman about to have twins. Is Colton excited?"

"He gets worse every single day. The overnight bag for the hospital has been packed and beside the front door for two weeks now."

Getting down from the bar stool wasn't any easier than climbing up had been. Feeling as graceful as a hippo, Sam managed to land on her feet without mishap. She followed Patricia over to a large corner booth.

"What about Luc?"

"Luc keeps sitting in the rocking chair in the

nursery. He says he's getting used to the chair before the baby comes."

Patricia grinned. Flanked on either side by a pregnant woman, she looked at each of them and then herself. "The best part about hanging out with the two of you is how you make me feel positively thin."

The bells on the front door jingled again.

"Hey, werewolf-man," someone called. "Done any good howling lately?"

Both Sam and Patricia turned to look. Charles Pentworth ducked his head, looking a bit sheepish.

"At least the mystery of the so-called werewolf got cleared up." Like Sam and Jewel, Patricia knew better, but she'd gone along with the story they'd concocted for the sake of peace. Luc had humanely trapped a large coyote, passing the animal off as the mystery wolf, before turning it over to the local game farm.

They'd also found and destroyed any remaining bear traps. Charles had set them, hoping to catch a werewolf.

Life was good.

"I have some news," Sam told them, unable to contain her excitement. "The adoption agency called again. I'm next on the list."

Patricia's eyes widened. "What are you going to do?"

Grinning, Sam shrugged. "I told them I was pregnant and to take me off the list. Some other prospective parents who've been waiting forever were given my spot. I can't think of a time when I've been happier."

"I can." Grinning, Patricia wagged her finger at her friend. "Let's see…what about when Luc asked you to marry him? Or at your wedding, when he read aloud the verses he'd written for you? Or the day you learned you were pregnant, after years of believing you couldn't have a child of your own?"

"Okay, okay." Laughing, Sam sipped her lemon-flavored water. "You're right. I'm a very lucky woman."

They all raised a glass of ice water in a toast.

Sam turned her attention to the menu, which Jewel was already avidly studying. "All I want to do these days is eat," Jewel said.

"Me, too." Sam patted her huge tummy. "This baby is always hungry. As a matter of fact—" The first pain hit like a tsunami. Gasping, she doubled over, her eyes watering. "Oh. My."

Patricia instantly grabbed her. "Are you—?"

"I think so. Yes."

As soon as Patricia's hand made contact, she snatched it back. "Ouch. That burns. You're doing it again."

"Sorry, but I have no control. Oh!" Another pain knifed through Sam's abdomen. "I think I'd better get to the hospital."

"Guys?" A look of shock crossed Jewel's face as she clutched her own abdomen. "You're not going to believe this, but I think I'm going to be joining you."

Six hours later

Luc paced the hospital corridor, stopping at Sam's room every time he made a complete circuit. He held her hand, helped her count, fed her ice chips, then had to pace the corridor again.

By the bed next to them, Colton, on the other hand, stayed at Jewel's side.

"Are you in here?" a familiar voice called. Carson stood in the doorway with Brenna and Lucy, Alex and Lyssa right behind them.

A second later, the doctor shooed everyone from the area. Only the husbands were allowed to remain.

Dr. Nettles had, at their request, flown to Texas to oversee Sam and Luc's child's birth. After all, the baby would be born a Halfling and, healer or not, would have unusual blood.

They couldn't take a chance on being discovered. Though most shifters had their children at home, Luc refused to risk Sam in any way. She was far too unique and special to him. Colton felt the same way about Jewel.

Jewel's twins were born first. A boy and a girl, they were both large, healthy babies with well-developed lungs.

Sam's eyes filled with tears when she heard their lusty cries.

Luc, thinking her tears were because of the pain, stopped his pacing and dropped into the chair at her side, taking her hand. "I love you," he said.

Too busy fighting a contraction to answer, she squeezed his fingers in response.

Their son was born with a full head of dark hair, shortly after midnight.

They named him Kyle.

Luc swore the baby grinned when he heard his name.

* * * * *

Turn the page for exciting previews of next month's Nocturne titles!

PERSECUTED by Lisa Childs
and
THE DARK GATE by Pamela Palmer

Available in April 2007,
wherever Silhouette Books are sold!

Persecuted
by
Lisa Childs

An exciting preview!

Chapter One

The muscles in Elena's arms strained as she struggled against the ropes binding her wrists behind her back. Coarse fibers bit into her skin, scratching so deeply that blood, warm and sticky, ran down her wrists and pooled in her palms.

She bit her lip, holding in a cry at the sting. But that pain was nothing in comparison to the heat of the flames springing up around her. Sweat ran down her face, nearly blinding her, but still she could see a man on the other side of the flames. A hood covered his head; a dark brown robe concealed his body. But his frame, his height and the breadth of his shoulders, identified him as male.

Others stood behind him in the shadows and smoke. They chanted, their voices rising above the hiss and crackle of the flames. "Exstinguo…veneficus…"

The words were unfamiliar, but she suspected they called her a witch.

"Nooo…" She wasn't a witch. The smoke choked her, cutting off her protest and her breath.

Her line of vision shifted, away from the cloaked figures, to the woman bound to the stake in the middle of the circle of flames. *Was* Elena the witch? The woman's hair was dark and curly, not blond like Elena's. The woman's eyes were dark and wide, not pale blue.

Uncaring of the pain, Elena continued to struggle, trying to free herself from the hold of the ropes, of the dream. Of the vision.

A scream tore from her throat as she kicked at the covers and bolted upright in bed. Shaking, she settled into the pillows piled against her headboard and gasped for breath, her lungs burning.

As the woman was burning…

Even awake Elena could see her, illuminated by a flash of lightning inside her mind. She squeezed her eyes shut and began a chant of her own, "It's just a dream. It's just a dream."

But she wasn't sleeping. She hardly ever slept anymore for fear of dreaming of torture and murder. The images rolled through her mind no matter where she was or what she was doing. They weren't like the "dreams" she'd had her whole life, the innocuous images of something someone might do or say a day or two after she'd dreamt it. These weren't little revelations of déjà vu. They were murder, and she was an eyewitness to the unspeakable horror.

She reached out, needing the comfort of strong arms to hold her, to protect her. But for the blankets tangled around her legs, the bed was empty and cold. Her husband no longer shared their room. She'd been the one to throw out his stuff after accusing him of cheating. Not even his tyrant of a boss would send him out of town as often as Kirk was gone.

Truthfully, she'd been gone a long time, too. Despite the fact she'd rarely left the house, she'd been absent from their marriage. She'd pushed him away. But why hadn't he fought for her, for them? Had he ever loved her or only her money? The hurt that pressed on her heart wasn't new, like an ache from an old injury rather than a fresh wound.

She fumbled with the switch on the lamp beside the bed and flooded the room with light. Real light. Not that eerie flash only inside her head. The warm glow of the bulb in the Tiffany lamp offered no comfort, either.

Although he denied the cheating and only moved as far as the guestroom, she knew Kirk was lying, but she hadn't told him how she'd gained her knowledge of his affair. She'd "seen" him with another woman. At first she'd passed those images off as she had her others, figments of her overactive imagination or products of stress or paranoia. Finally she'd forced herself to face the truth about her sham of a marriage…and herself.

She didn't love Kirk; maybe she never had, because she'd never trusted him enough to tell him anything about her past or herself. During college, their relationship was mostly superficial and fun, things that Elena's life had never been. But their relationship had never really deepened, despite marriage, despite the beautiful four-year-old daughter they shared, and it had stopped being fun a long time ago. Sick of all the lies, his and hers, she'd finally filed for divorce.

For so long Elena hadn't been able to discern truth from fiction. Although she hadn't seen her mother in twenty years, she could hear her lilting voice echoing in her head with the words of a gypsy proverb, *There are such things as false truths and honest lies.*

When she'd been taken away from her mother two decades ago, she had also been separated from her younger half-sisters. She'd only recently reconnected with Ariel. Elena had been twelve, Ariel nine and their youngest sister, Irina, just four when social services had taken them away from their mother. They'd never seen Mother again. Alive.

Ariel had seen her dead, though. Her sister could see people after they passed away. She hadn't wanted to see Elena and Irina for the first time in two decades the way she had their mother, so she'd searched for her sisters to warn them that someone had started a witch hunt. She hadn't found Irina yet, and had only stumbled across Elena by accident.

But Elena had already known about the witch hunt because of her dreams. She'd fought so hard to suppress her visions, to convince herself that they weren't real. When her sister had found her, Elena had had to admit to the truth, if only to herself.

The visions were why Elena was cursed, not the three-hundred-and-fifty-year-old vendetta that had started the first witch hunt. One of Elena's Durikken ancestors had been accused of killing the female members of the McGregor family and was burned at the stake. But like Elena, she'd seen her future and urged her daughter to run. That child, for whom Elena was named, had found safety, and she'd continued the Durikken legacy, passing onto her children the special abilities that people mistook for witchcraft.

Now someone else had resurrected the vendetta that Eli McGregor had begun three and a half centuries ago, of ritualistically killing all witches. Elena had dreamed, sleeping and awake, of his murders. While she *saw* his victims, she hadn't seen the killer; she couldn't identify *him*. Helplessness and frustration churned in her stomach, gnawing at the lining like ulcers.

She didn't want to remember those horrifying images.

She didn't want to be a witch.

With that thought firmly in mind, Elena tried to get back to sleep. She tossed and turned, until finally, sleep found her…and she relaxed.

Elena had no idea how long she'd been asleep when moist lips touched her shoulder, gliding over the bare skin. Her pulse quickening, she murmured and shifted against the bed, struggling to awaken. She dragged in a deep breath, the scent of citrus soap and musk.

This was not her husband joining her in bed. He wasn't even down the hall tonight; he was out of town. But when he'd been around, he hadn't touched her, not for a long time. From the way he'd started looking at her, with uneasiness and a trace of fear, he might have figured out that his wife wasn't normal. Perhaps he'd picked up clues from her nightmares, or from the things she knew before he told her.

The lips moved, nibbling along her shoulder to her neck. The brush of moist, hot breath raised goose bumps along her skin. The blanket lowered, pushed aside by impatient hands. Then those strong, clever hands ran over her body, skimming down her arms, then around her waist and over her hips. Sometime during the night, even though the air blowing through her windows was cool in mid-May in western Michigan, she had removed her nightgown. Nothing separated her skin from his as his body brushed against hers.

"Elena," a deep voice whispered in her ear, his hot breath stirring her hair and her senses. "You're ready for me."

Excitement pulsed in her veins, and she opened her eyes, staring up into his face as he leaned over her. Desire had darkened his eyes so that only a thin circle of green rimmed his enlarged pupils. A muscle jumped in his cheek, shadowed with the beard clinging to his square jaw.

"Elena, I want you." His biceps bulged as he braced his arms on the mattress on either side of her, trapping her beneath the long, hard length of his body. His voice deepened to a throaty growl as he told her, "I want to bury myself so deep inside you that you'll feel me forever as a part of you."

"You're already part of me," she murmured.

His were the arms she'd instinctively sought earlier, when the horrifying dream had awakened her. She turned to *him* for comfort and protection. And for *this*, for the passion that pounded like a drum in her heart, heating her skin and melting her muscles so that she flowed beneath him, fitting herself to the hard lines of his body.

His chest tempted her, wide and muscular with soft, black hair that grew thinner as it arrowed down, over his washboard stomach. Some of the hair dusted his muscular legs, tickling hers, as he entwined them.

He was naked and ready. And so was she.

Her stomach quivering with anticipation, she reached up, twining her arms around his back, pulling him closer. But his weight didn't settle hot and heavy against her. Her arms moved through empty space, flailing the covers aside as she moved restlessly in her bed, empty but for her.

For the second time that night she bolted upright, panting for breath, her lungs burning with the struggle for air, as she awakened from a dream.

Just a dream.

This was no vision of the future, for there could be no future between Elena and her dream lover. Unlike the killer, she'd seen this man's face; she knew him, and she wished she didn't.

He might not be the killer, but to Elena, he was just as big a threat, if not to her life, to her heart. His were the last arms in which she would find comfort or protection. With a man like him, she'd only find more heartache and danger.

The Dark Gate
by
Pamela Palmer

An exciting preview!

Chapter 1

"Three assaults in five days, more than a dozen bystanders and no one remembers a thing. *How in the hell is he doing it?*"

Metropolitan Police Detective Jack Hallihan paced the aft deck of the small cabin cruiser docked on the Potomac River in downtown Washington, D.C., his steps echoing his frustration. A jet roared overhead, making its final approach into Reagan National, while the summer sun beat down on the back of his neck, sending sweat rolling between his shoulder blades. He was running out of time.

"He's gotta be knocking 'em out, Jack." Duke, a fellow detective and the wiry dark-skinned owner of the boat, tipped his baseball cap to shield his eyes from the afternoon sun even as his head turned, his gaze following the progress of a pair of young women strolling down the dock in bikini tops and short-shorts. "What's up, ladies?"

The voices in Jack's head surged suddenly, unintelligible voices that filled his head night and day and had for as long as he could remember. He clenched his teeth and dug his fingers into his dark hair, pressing his fingers to his scalp, trying to quiet the ceaseless chatter, if only a little.

"You okay, man?" Henry Jefferson, Jack's partner of ten years, eyed him with concern from the second deck chair as he rolled a cold Budweiser across a forehead several shades darker than Duke's. Henry was as tall as Jack, but no longer lean. Too many years of his wife, Mei's, fried egg rolls had softened him around the middle. There was nothing soft about the gaze he leveled on Jack. "You need to see someone about those headaches of yours."

Jack snatched his hand from his head. *Damn.* The last thing he needed was to bring attention to his worsening condition. No one knew he suffered from the same madness that destroyed his father. If he had his way, no one ever would.

"It's just the heat," he told his friend. If only. Hell, he'd be happy if they were just headaches. Sometimes he felt as though he lived in the middle of a raucous party that never ended, a party where everyone spoke Bulgarian, or Mongolian, or some other language he would never understand. Usually he could tamp down the noise so it didn't overwhelm his mind, like moving the party into the next room. But the past couple of weeks the voices had been all but shouting in his ears.

He pulled the discussion back to the problem at hand, a mysterious rapist terrorizing the Dupont Circle neighborhood of D.C. "In each of the three cases, multiple victims were knocked unconscious by some unknown means to awaken simultaneously a short while later—estimated at anywhere from fifteen to thirty minutes. In each case, one young woman among them woke to find her clothing partially removed and blood and semen between her legs. In each case, no one, including the assault victim, remembered anything to help us identify the attacker and solve this case."

"It makes no sense," Duke said. "How is he

knocking them out before they ever get a look at him?"

"We need those tox reports," Jack said. "He's got to be using some kind of gas or drug."

The muscle in Henry's jaw visibly tightened. "I want his ass *now*, before he hurts another girl. The last assault victim was just eighteen years old. Barely more than a kid."

Henry's own daughter, Sabrina, was only a handful of years younger. She and her brother were belowdeck even now. Henry wasn't leaving her home alone. He wasn't taking any chances. Jack didn't blame him a bit.

"And what does the theft at the Smithsonian have to do with all this?" Henry wondered out loud. During the first attack, an ancient stone amulet had been stolen.

"What did you find out about this *Stone of Ezrie?*" he asked his friend. But Duke's gaze was firmly fixed on a well-endowed teen making her way along the dock.

Henry gave Duke's shoulder a hard slug. "Stay in the game, man. We want to know what you learned."

Duke released a frustrated sigh. "It's Sunday. Even cops need a day off."

"Not when girls are being attacked," Henry growled.

"Yeah, okay." Duke pulled out his wallet and removed a small paper photo. "*The Stone of Ezrie.*"

Jack took the piece of paper and held it for Henry to see. The photo revealed a sky-blue, teardrop-shaped stone hanging from a simple silver chain. Engraved on the surface of the stone was a seven-point star.

"Why would anyone want this thing?" Henry asked, echoing Jack's own thoughts. "What kind of rock is it, anyway?"

Duke shrugged. "Nothing valuable. The Smithsonian dude didn't know why anyone would steal it. There were better things all around. The only thing this rock has going for it is some quack legend. Something about it being the key that opens the gates to Ezrie."

Henry lifted a thick brow. "What's Ezrie?"

"Don't know. It's all bogus, man. Prime bogus. There ain't no way to solve this case or to catch the perp until the son of a bitch screws up and leaves us a witness or clue. We've been over everything a dozen times." Duke reached for another beer. "*I* need a day off, even if you two don't. So no more talk about work. How 'bout them Nationals, huh?"

Jack took a long drink of Coke, letting it fizz on his tongue as impatience boiled under his skin. He didn't have time for talk of baseball. He'd managed to push the voices back, but for how long? How much longer until he couldn't control them at all?

He had to solve this case while he still had the mental strength to do it, before the voices became too much to bear and he ended up like his *dad*— an alcoholic with a gun in his mouth.

The silken sound of a woman's laughter yanked him out of his dark musings, stealing every thought from his head. His gaze snapped to the houseboat in the next slip as a tall, slender blonde in nice pants and a trim sleeveless sweater emerged from the door of the boat, holding a cell phone to her ear. She was laughing as she stepped outside, her chin-length hair glowing golden in the summer sunshine.

Jack swallowed. "Who's that?"

"Larsen Vale. Bleeding-heart lawyer and Ice Bitch extraordinaire. Forget about her. She don't give it up for no man." Duke's words were too loud for the small distance between the boats, but he didn't seem to care.

The woman glanced up. The laughter drained from her features as though someone had pulled a plug. All emotion fled. Her gaze slid over the men, one after the other, as if they were nothing more than inanimate objects unworthy of her notice… until her gaze slammed into Jack's. His heart bucked in his chest, a physical jolt like he'd been sucker-punched. She held his gaze, then dropped it, shattering it as she turned away.

She clicked her cell phone closed and started across the boat's narrow deck with quick, confident strides, a briefcase swinging at her side. Without another glance his way, she hopped lightly onto the dock and strode away.

Jack exhaled. "Wow."

"She's cold, dude," Duke insisted. "Ice cold. Don't waste your time."

"Dad." Henry's ten-year-old son, David, ran up the stairs from below, making enough noise for three kids despite his slight build. "When are we sailing?"

"You don't sail a motorboat, moron." His sister, Sabrina, flounced up the stairs behind him.

"Sorry, you two. We're not taking the boat out," Henry told his kids. "This is a marina party, not a river cruise."

"What party?" David asked. "This is boring."

"*David…*"

Jack set his half-empty Coke can on the railing.

"Who's up for a walk?" He had too much on his mind to make small talk. If he had to take the afternoon off, he'd rather spend his time with the kids, anyway. He sure as hell wouldn't have any of his own. Not after what his dad had put his own family through.

"Me, Uncle Jack, me," David exclaimed, jumping up and down. "Can I get the football out of the car, Dad?"

Henry nodded and Jack turned to Sabrina. "You coming, beautiful?" At fourteen, the girl was already showing signs of the heartbreaker she was destined to become.

He held his breath, waiting for her reply, wondering if this would be the time she'd finally grown too cool to have anything to do with her "uncle" Jack. But she flashed him a smile full of braces and youthful exuberance, and he knew today wasn't that day. They found a patch of grass in front of the marina to pass the football.

"You suck," Sabrina shouted as David ran for the ball he'd missed.

"*You* suck," the boy called back, laughing. If there was a natural athlete lurking in the kid somewhere, he had yet to show himself. David grabbed the ball and started running toward them.

Jack held up his hands. "Throw it, pal." But the boy kept running. Jack laughed, happier out here with these two than he'd been in weeks.

"Throw it, David." Sabrina waved her hands in the air.

The boy finally heaved the football, getting a nice spiral on it, at last. Unfortunately his aim was off. Way off. The ball sailed directly at the door of the marina office and the woman exiting through it—Larsen Vale.

Jack cringed as the ball hit her square in the arm, knocking her briefcase out of her hand. The briefcase hit the wall and clattered to the sidewalk, snapping open. Papers spilled everywhere.

Hell. She was going to tear the kid to pieces. As David started toward her in his loping run, Jack headed after him, determined to save him from a tongue-lashing that would make his sister's impatient comments sound like sweet nothings.

"Sorry," David called good-naturedly as he approached the she-devil.

The woman picked up the ball. To Jack's amazement she gave David a rueful smile and cocked her arm as if to throw it.

"Go long," she told him.

David grinned and started running. The woman

threw an admirable pass with only a slight wobble, right into the boy's arms.

"Yesss!" David did his own little version of the touchdown shuffle.

Jack looked at Larsen Vale thoughtfully as she knelt to gather up her papers. He'd heard her name before today. He knew she'd earned herself a reputation for ruthlessness in the courtroom, particularly in defense of women abused by their high-profile husbands. Duke wasn't the only one who called her the Ice Bitch. Yet she'd just been exceedingly kind in a situation that would have provoked most people to anger.

Jack joined her. "Let me give you a hand with those." He knelt beside her and began picking up the loose papers. He'd thought her attractive on the boat. This close, she was stunning. Her mouth was wide and lush, perfectly framed by a strong, stubborn jaw. Her eyes had a natural, heavy-lidded appearance that was sexy as hell. And her skin was lightly tanned and flawlessly smooth.

Heat tightened things low in his body. He couldn't remember the last time he'd been hit with this kind of lust at first sight. Too bad she was ignoring him.

"Thanks for being patient with David. He's a little careless sometimes."

She looked up and gave him the same expressionless look she had on the boat. Her eyes were a clear golden-brown beneath a thin layer of frost.

"Were you afraid I'd shatter him with my ice wand?"

Jack winced. So she'd heard Duke's comment. "You had a right to be angry with him. I appreciate your patience."

She stopped in her gathering and glanced toward the kids. "He was just being a boy."

"Yeah. I apologize for my friend's rudeness back there, too. His comments were out of line." Jack tapped the papers he'd collected on the sidewalk to neaten the stack. "He's a little too cocksure of his success with women." He handed the stack to her and their fingers brushed. A bare slide of flesh on flesh.

Inexplicably the chatter in his head went silent. *Silent.* For the first time in...*forever.*

She jerked, dropping the papers. "Damn."

The voices rushed back as if they'd never left at all. Jack's heart slammed in his chest. Had he imagined it?

She gathered up the last of the papers and put them back in her expensive-looking briefcase. As she started to close the lid, the breeze caught a loose sheet. Jack grabbed for it at the same time she did. Their hands brushed again.

Silence. It was her.

Larsen Vale clicked her briefcase shut and rose. She met his gaze, briefly, as dispassionately as before. "Thanks," she said, and turned away.

Jack stared after her, stunned. *She'd quieted the voices.*

Hope roared through his veins like a flood through a parched gully. *She'd quieted the damn voices.*

She was his salvation. *His cure.*

nocturne™

**An ancient evil has found its way back to our world....
And the only ones who can stop it don't know it exists.**

Larsen Vale has a secret: she sees things.
Terrible things. Deadly things. Haunted and
afraid, she trusts no one, not even Jack, the
handsome detective she is helping on a puzzling
case. But time is running out. If Larsen and Jack
can't learn to trust each other, the Gate will be
opened—and the world will be forever changed....

THE DARK GATE

PAMELA PALMER

On sale April.

SNA07LC

HARLEQUIN® *Romance*®

presents a brand-new trilogy by

PATRICIA THAYER

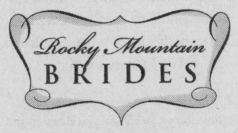

Rocky Mountain B R I D E S

Three sisters come home to wed.

In April don't miss

Raising the Rancher's Family,

followed by

The Sheriff's Pregnant Wife,

on sale May 2007,

and

A Mother for the Tycoon's Child,

on sale June 2007.

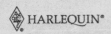

EVERLASTING LOVE™

Every great love has a story to tell™

Available March 27

And look for
The Marriage Bed by **Judith Arnold**
and
Family Stories by **Tessa Mcdermid,**
from Harlequin® Everlasting Love™
this May.

If you're a romantic at heart, you'll definitely
want to read this new series. Pick up a book today!